ONE LITTLE HEARTBREAK

AVERY MAXWELL

THE BEST OF US LLC

Copyright © 2021 by Avery Maxwell

All rights reserved.

No part of this book may be reproduced in any form or by any electronic or mechanical means, including information storage and retrieval systems, without written permission from the author, except for the use of brief quotations in a book review.

❦ Created with Vellum

To all my readers that support me unconditionally, I thank you.

A NOTE FROM AVERY

The Westbrooks are a large family you first met in The Westbrooks: Broken Hearts Series. You were introduced to Seth, Ashton, Halton, Colton and Easton in those books, and now you get their stories.

If you would like to meet them from the beginning, read:
Cross My Heart: Dexter & Lanie
Beat of My Heart: Trevor & Julia
Saving His Heart: Preston Westbrook & Emory
Romancing His Heart: Loki & Sloane

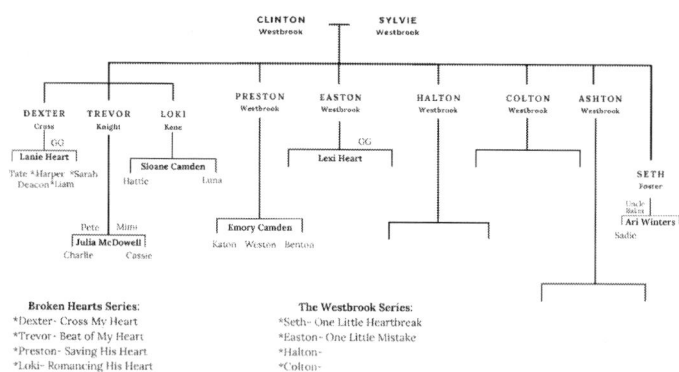

CHAPTER 1

SETH

"Daddy? Why does Nanna Sylvie live in a castle?"

I catch Sadie's reflection in the rearview mirror. The sun shimmers on her blonde, curly hair while she sits strapped into her car seat. The pink tulle from her princess dress spills out over the sides like the icing of a cupcake. Like so many times recently, I'm reminded of her mother.

Oh, Rebecca. What am I going to do with our little girl without you here?

"Nanna Sylvie doesn't live in a castle, sweetheart."

Okay, to be fair, I thought the same thing the first time I rolled up to the Westbrook compound.

"It's more of a mansion," I explain.

I know where this question will lead, but thankfully, the large, iron gates emblazoned with WB on the front open just in time.

"We're here, we're here," my little girl squeals while clapping her hands, blonde curls bouncing with the effort. "Let me outta here, Daddy! I gots to find my Uncle Ash. He's waitin for me, I'm sure."

Internally, I grimace. Ashton has been my friend for a long time, and now he's also my business partner. We worked together in a recently defunct top-secret government agency called SIA—Select Intelligence Agency. Our friend, Loki, who Ashton's mother adopted, brought us all together.

A few weeks ago, our worlds came crashing down when we were ambushed. Ash was the only civilian, and they brutally tortured him. His face now bears a scar, but it's the mark it left on his soul we are all concerned about. My daughter has made it her mission to kiss those booboos away. A part of me dies every time she explains her reasoning.

"We couldn't kiss Mommy's booboo's because they were on the inside. Uncle Ash is so lucky 'cause his are right there. Right where I can kiss them every day."

Swallowing thickly, I turn off the engine and round the car to unbuckle her. Sadie is tiny for her age, much like her mother, so she still needs the four-point harness. Luckily, she doesn't complain about it too much.

"I'm sure Uncle Ash is excited to see you, sweetheart. Just remember, he still has booboos on the inside, too, so you need to be careful about jumping on him."

She stares at me as if I grew an extra head. "Daddy, I knows it. I'm a very good nurse, you know?"

That makes me smile. "Yes, baby, I know. Come on. Nanna Sylvie's waiting."

What she's waiting for, I don't have a clue. Sometime in the last year, Sylvie Westbrook, the matriarch of the Westbrook empire, has added to her collection of boys. Apparently, five biological sons were not enough because years ago, she took in three of her eldest son, Preston's, friends as her own. I'm the most recent addition to her lineup.

I'm not sure what to make of that. My parents washed

their hands of me the second I turned eighteen and have never looked back. I was the quintessential "oops" baby. But Sylvie has a special way about her, and when she says you're family, there's no refuting it. Secretly, it's growing on me. I've never had a large family of my own, and this crazy bunch of billionaires is teaching me that family is what you make it.

Did I forget to mention that part? They're all billionaires. I'm still not used to it. Ash, Loki, and I have been in business for less than a month, and the direct deposit that hit my account yesterday had me falling out of my chair. Literally. When I called the bank, they confirmed the amount was correct.

Loki and Ashton made me a partner in our new company, even though I didn't have the capital to invest. When I questioned them about the deposit, they assured me that was after I had made the monthly buy-in payment.

"We take care of family, Seth. You're family by choice. Family by blood is a coincidence, not a requirement for us. Get used to it," Ashton had wheezed over the phone. The assholes who attacked us kicked in his vocal cords during our nightmare, and his voice will never be the same.

"When we made you a partner, we knew you didn't have the capital to invest. So every month, your deposit reflects income minus a buy-in payment," Loki had assured.

I've never had so much money at once in all my life. Knowing this happens monthly will take some getting used to. Not that I'm complaining, it's just a different world.

Sadie rips me from the memory as she goes running past, pink tulle flowing in the breeze. She insisted on wearing the princess dress to make Uncle Ash happy. I don't know if he's prepared for the whirlwind that is princess Sadie, but she's on a mission to find him, and she has a one-track mind.

Jogging to catch up, I meet her at the door. Just as I'm about to knock, it opens wide. Sylvie stands on the threshold, looking as if she just walked out of a Vineyard Vines catalog. Her pink cardigan that's tied around her shoulders matches Sadie's tulle, and it doesn't go unnoticed by my little girl.

"Oh, Nanna Sylvie, we match! We match!" Sadie jumps from foot to foot until Sylvie opens her arms wide for a hug. As if on cue, Sadie launches herself at the older woman. She's never had a grandmother, and I couldn't ask for a better substitute than Sylvie Westbrook.

"Is he here, Nanna Sylvie? Is he here yet?" The excitement in Sadie's voice is infectious, and Sylvie's beaming smile confirms my suspicions.

"He is, dear. He's in the library."

"He's waiting for me, isn't he?" Sadie asks excitedly.

Sylvie looks at me and winks. "He is most definitely waiting for you, princess Sadie." She doesn't even get the sentence out before Sadie takes off at a dead run.

"Sadie," I scold.

"Oh, Seth, let her go. It's good for Ashton. She brings him a desperately needed light right now. Actually, after I speak to you boys—"

We're interrupted by Preston breezing past me. He pauses to give me a fist bump and kisses his mother on the cheek. Suave is the best way to describe him with his dark hair and bright blue eyes. He looks the part of a young billionaire.

"Where are the boys?" he asks, just before he howls like an animal.

I'm still shocked every time his howl is met with three more. I'm pretty sure I even hear Sadie's sweet voice chime in, and I roll my eyes.

"Get used to it, man. You're part of the chaos now," he says, smirking. 'Welcome to the chaos' is a chant his father started when they were young. It's now the family motto.

Giving in, I raise my fist to meet his as he yells, "Welcome to the chaos." I repeat the sentiment, and he wanders off in search of his brothers.

Sylvie wraps her arm in mine and leads me down the hall. "You'll get used to the pack, Seth. You're one of us now."

"So everyone keeps reminding me," I grumble. It's not that I'm ungrateful, but I'm unsure how to handle this big family.

"As I was saying, after I speak to you boys, I have a special request for Sadie. Just keep an open mind, okay?"

My spine prickles at her choice of words. Until recently, Sadie was all I had. Having other people care for her, love her, and want to protect her as if she's theirs is unfamiliar territory for me. She and I have been on our own for over two years now, but I still miss her mother every single day.

Sylvie pulls me down to meet her eyes and kisses me on the cheek. "It's nothing to worry about, Seth. You and Sadie are our family now, and we take care of our own. I just like spending time with her. And, someone needs her special brand of sunshine more than anyone I know." She nods her head to the left, and I follow her line of vision.

Propped up in a portable hospital bed is Ashton. Tucked into his side, reading him a book, is Sadie. I tear my gaze away quickly—the guilt over Ashton's condition threatening to cause a scene.

Sylvie pats my shoulder. "Take a seat. I'll get right to the point."

We hear the front door chime, announcing someone has entered the house, and I see Ashton tense. His brother, Colton, is completely oblivious and jumps off the couch at the sound.

"Yes! I'm getting the asshat this time," Colt laughs, standing out of sight to the side of the large, oak door.

"Colton Westbrook, don't you da—

Sylvie's words are cut off as Loki rounds the corner just as Colt jumps out and screams.

Loki, ex-military, lashes out fast and fierce with a quick jab to Colton's nose. Blood erupts everywhere.

"Jesus Christ, Colt. What the fuck are you doing?" Loki bellows. "We're not ten year olds anymore, you asshole." Even as he speaks, he's pinching Colt's nose and tipping his head back.

"Not again," Sylvie grumbles, scurrying to grab a towel. I stand frozen to my spot, gaping like a fish. "And watch your language, boys."

"What the hell was that?" I mumble.

Another Westbrook brother, Halton, appears at my side. "That was Colton. He suffers from the Peter Pan syndrome," he growls.

I'm always amazed by how similar the brothers look when their attitudes couldn't be more different. I've learned, over time, that Halt isn't really a talker or overly friendly, but he always has your back.

I stand stock-still as the chaos literally engulfs the room. Then, as quickly as it started, Sylvie has her animals under control.

"Sit," she orders, with more authority than I've ever heard from her. Suddenly, I can see how she kept these boys in line all these years.

Every grown man in the room complies immediately. She spares a disapproving scowl at Colton, then composes herself and addresses the room.

"I need you boys to go to Vermont. The plane leaves in two hours. Everything you'll need will already be on board."

I peer left, then right. No one seems put off by this odd statement.

What does she mean we need to go to Vermont? For what?

"Oh, dear. Let me explain, Seth. Easton is still there, helping Lexi and her grandmother, GG, with the mountain lodge. Apparently, something has come up with who can develop one side of the mountain, and the Macombs arrived last week."

"What the hell?" Preston barks, standing suddenly. "Why the—"

"Language, Preston," Sylvie scolds again, nodding toward Sadie.

"Sorry," he grumbles. "But why would the Macombs show up in that tiny town? It makes no sense."

"If they got word East has been there for a while, they likely think they're missing out on something big. My guess is if they think the mountain is up for grabs, they're there to outbid East," Halton growls.

"Shit," Loki murmurs, and Sylvie slaps his hand like a toddler. "Sylvie, I've got—"

"Yes, I know," she interrupts. "you've been through a lot recently. But, if the boys call and need you, I expect you to show up." Her tone leaves no room for debate.

"Of course," he replies.

It was Loki's future wife that saved us from the brutal attacks we were enduring just a short time ago. Sloane is an amazing woman and perfect for Loki, but he has his work cut out for himself with her.

"Mom, Emory and I are ... well, we're meeting with fertility doctors." Preston pinches the back of his neck.

Sylvie crosses the room and pats his cheek. "I know, Pres. I talked to Emory yesterday. It's okay. You take care of your wife. You're on a difficult journey, and she'll need you for all the doctor's appointments, but be ready for the call. If your brothers need you, I expect you to help in any way you can. Lexi and GG are part of our family, too."

He nods in understanding. "I will."

I had no idea they were even trying for a baby. *After the journey they've taken, they deserve a happy ending more than anyone I know. Jesus, his wife, Emory, is the reason Preston and Loki are both alive right now.*

Sylvie turns to the rest of us. "That leaves Colton, Halt, and Seth," she says happily.

I glance around the room, dumbfounded. What the hell does she expect me to do?

"Ah, Sylvie? I have Sadie and—"

"And that's what I wanted to talk to you about. I was hoping Sadie could stay with Ash and me for the week." Her smile is too broad. I swear she's outshining the sun right now.

Turning to my left, I see Ashton cradling Sadie in the small bed, her head resting on his chest. He looks content and calm—something that has eluded him in the weeks since our attack, and Sylvie's plan suddenly becomes crystal clear. Sadie pulls Ash from the darkness.

"She's a lot of work," I offer.

"Pfft. Seth, I raised five boys, plus three of their friends. I can handle one princess. In fact, it will be fun for all of us." The sincerity shows in her eyes, and I nod my consent.

That's how, two hours later, I board a tiny, private plane called The Beaver with Halton growling his displeasure and Colt holding a bag of ice to his face.

"I think Loki broke my nose," he says in shock. "Can you believe that?"

"Well, you did jump out and scare the shit out of an ex-military special agent who was recently held hostage, so …"

"Jesus, when you put it that way, it doesn't sound so good," he mumbles.

"Not so much, no." I chuckle.

I watch as they take their seats, and finally, I join them. It's not the first time I have flown on a Westbrook private plane, and even though this one is much smaller, I'm not any more comfortable now than I was the first time.

"It gets easier," Halton grumbles.

"What does?"

"Feeling like you belong." He places his AirPods in his ears, ending the conversation, and I mull over his words. I'm fairly confident I'll never feel like I belong in this world, but I'll try harder to appreciate it.

Three hours later, we touch down in West Burke, Vermont, on the tiniest grass runway I've ever seen, and I can't help but wonder what kind of shitshow I'm walking into.

CHAPTER 2

ARI

"Ari, dear? Do you think we can make a little extra room in the case for me? I hear GG is bringing another round of handsome rich men to town. I want to make sure I have enough of these sexy treats to keep those hot specimens coming back for more." Uncle Baker winks, and I have to hold my stomach so it doesn't revolt.

I adore GG—everyone in this town does—but the last round of billionaires to roll through here are a bunch of assholes. The only one I can tolerate is Easton, and that's because he's a grumpy bastard who keeps to himself. Or at least he did until Lexi gave him a makeover.

"Uncle Baker, I really don't think you should encourage them. The latest group to come through here has been terrible."

Uncle Baker, with his flair for drama, splutters before speaking. "Okay, Ari, I'll give you that. They have not taken to small-town life the way I'd hoped, but it's not our place to judge."

"What do you mean, it isn't our place to judge? You're the mayor, and you're planning to sell GG's mountain to one of them. I'd say that gives us a lot of room to judge. If we sell it to the wrong group, it could be disastrous for the town."

Every morning at five a.m., we have this conversation when he brings in his baked goods from his shop next door. He has run the Bossy Baker for as long as I have been alive. He takes his roles, both as mayor and as the town baker, very seriously. So seriously, in fact, he changed his last name from Raymond to Baker about twenty years ago.

"That is why, my dear Ari, we will have a town meeting at Summerfest to cast a vote. Just imagine the draw it will bring. All those sexy billionaires milling about? I'm sure it will be the event of the decade."

"I don't see why they would attract so much attention," I grumble.

He sucks in so much air that he wheezes until the end. "Ari Winters. Have you not seen the pictures of the Westbrook brothers? Each one is hotter than the next. Ferguson and I were just admiring GG's last installment in the Town Cryer."

The Town Cryer is GG's baby. For an eighty-year-old woman, her texting skills are on point. As soon as she found out gossip traveled faster by text, she created a town-wide thread. She even got Uncle Baker to approve it as a safety measure, so everyone in town automatically receives the notifications. I'm not sure about its legality, but this town has always made its own rules.

"Fine, but what about that other group? The Macombs? They walk in here like they own the place, and they're rude," I hiss.

"Ari?" my stepmother barks from the back stairs. "What is all that noise down there? Your sisters and I are trying to sleep. Show a little respect and keep quiet! The last thing you want is for me to be too tired to deal with this shop and have to sell it."

"Oh, for Pete's sake, Virginia. Shut your trap," Uncle

Baker snaps, then lowers his voice. "Ari, why do you put up with this shit?"

"John Baker, do not speak to me that way in my own home."

He marches to the back stairs and points his finger at her wildly. His salt and pepper hair, which is always a smidge too long, flaps in his wake. His red dhoti flows behind him in his rush to the stairs.

Half Irish and half Indian, he got his coloring from his father—dark hair, and the fairest Irish skin I've ever seen. Yet, he still prefers the clothing from his mother's home country. He says it makes him feel close to her, even though she's been gone for years. It's something I'm starting to understand now that my own parents are gone. I love Uncle Baker more than anything, but he is quite the sight around town, even I can admit that.

"For the last time, Vagina, this building belonged to Ari's mother, Lilly, and as soon as I can figure out the legalese, I'm kicking your ass to the street."

Virginia gasps and slams her door.

Sighing, I adjust the pastry case to accommodate his ridiculous amount of treats.

"You know that only makes it worse for me, right?" Although I love his protectiveness, Virginia will probably find a way to take her humiliation out on me.

Rounding the counter, he places his hands on my shoulders. "Ari, your dad was my best friend for over forty years. He was my childhood hero who always stuck up for me when others made fun of me for being *too feminine*. That was a thing back then, you know?"

I nod, thankful we've come so far, but I know some people still don't respect Uncle Baker for his choices. He and his lifelong partner, Uncle Ferguson, bring so much joy to everyone they meet. I hate knowing people still can't let love be. We have a mutual protective streak for each other now that my parents are gone, and they're truly the only family I have left.

"Ian would be so pissed off to see the way you're treated now. Why don't you stick up for yourself, sweetheart? I know there's more to the story than you're telling me. Like why the hell are you living in that shed out back instead of the room your mother designed for you?"

My throat tightens, thinking about my room. My mother was an amazing artist and had painted murals on every wall of my room—it was my safe place for so many years.

"Virginia gave it to Brittany because Tiffany didn't want to share a room anymore. Th-They painted over my murals." My throat catches, and I have to look away as tears threaten once again.

"That goddamn bitch," he bellows. "When the hell did she do that? And where did she expect you to go?"

"I-I don't know. It doesn't matter," I say, attempting to pull away from him before the emotions overwhelm me.

"Sweetheart, I thought you moved out there because you wanted some privacy. Why didn't you come to me? You know you are always welcome with Fergie and me." I can hear the tears in his eyes without ever glancing up.

"Because …" I start, unsure of how much to tell him. "Because I know if I'm not here to look after Daddy's legacy, she'll ruin it all. This building is all I have left of Mom. Virginia told Daddy she put all my mother's things in storage for me when they got married, but the truth is, she sent it all to the dump."

Uncle Baker, a pacifist by nature, looks ready to murder someone. "Ari, this is a historical building. The town bylaws state she cannot sell it without my approval. Let me help you here, please."

"I-I'm not sure where to even start. She pays me less than five dollars an hour …"

"What do you mean? Where the hell does all the money go?"

Looking to the ceiling, I recall weekly shopping trips, visits to the spa, and the daily shipments from Amazon.

"No, sweetheart. This is not okay. How do you even afford your art supplies with that measly amount? Is that why you're losing so much weight? Are you not eating? How the hell didn't I know any of this sooner?"

I sigh. Uncle Baker didn't know because I didn't want him to, but I'm getting tired, and I feel my emotional state slipping. My mother suffered from depression, and I know it can be hereditary, so I'm aware I need to make some changes. I'm just scared of the repercussions.

"I eat, uncle Baker. I do the store inventory," I whisper. "I take what I need to get by." I hate that it makes me feel like a criminal, but I consider it payment for all my work when the store is closed.

"The general store was Ian's dream, baby girl, not yours. He never expected you to put your life on hold to keep it going."

I swallow sandpaper and acknowledge that he's right. "I-I know. But it's all I have left of him."

Strong arms wrap around me so tightly I choke on air trapped in my lungs. "You're twenty-four, Ari. You should be out having fun with friends, not slaving away in a country store twenty hours a day. We will make some changes, young lady, and first up is figuring out how to get this building back into your name. Leave it to me, Ari. I've got you … always."

I choke up at his declaration, but I've read over my father's will. I don't believe anyone can help me at this point.

CHAPTER 3

SETH

"So, what you're telling us is Macomb found out you were here, and now he's trying to buy the backside of GG's mountain?" Colt asks.

"Pretty much," East says from his perch in the corner.

"Why the hell do you look like you just walked out of a thrift shop?" Halton grumbles.

"Because I did. I don't want to talk about it," East barks.

Glancing around the room, I see Lexi smirking, and I know she had something to do with his outfit.

"I told him if he was going to stay here, he had to at least try to blend in. It's the only way the town will vote for us at Summerfest. And, th-they," her voice breaks, "have to vote for us."

"Don't worry, Lex. We got this." Colt hugs her, and Easton growls.

I don't know who's grumpier, Easton or Halt, but you'd think their life had been full of hardship instead of being a couple of rich, good looking assholes.

"The town loves GG. Why would they vote any other way?" Halt mutters.

"The town does love her, but it's divided. We need jobs

brought to the area, and Macomb is promising that," Lexi explains.

"We're on it," Colt says gently. His arm is still draped over her shoulder. He knows he's pissing off Easton, and he's doing it on purpose. Whatever is going on between East and Lexi is making the tension in the room dense. "What do you need us to do?"

"You're the President of Westbrook Marketing, Colt. We need you to spin our family so we can get GG's mountain back. Halton, we need you to work on some numbers. And, Seth? We need you to work the town," Easton growls.

Shocked, I peer up to see if he's joking. He's not. "Ah, I'm not exactly the most personable guy, East. Wouldn't Colton be better suited for that?"

"Yes," Lexi explains. "And, he'll help after he has a plan in place, but until then, we're hoping you can be the face of The Westbrook Group."

"But, I'm not a Westbrook." I stare at them all, stunned.

Colton laughs. "We welcomed you to the chaos, man. You're as good as one of us now."

"Fuck." The Westbrooks are the most openly loving family I've ever encountered. It makes me uncomfortable.

"You'll want to start at the general store," Lexi informs me. "GG goes down there every morning during rush hour to read cards."

A collective groan echoes through the room.

"As long as she doesn't pull my cards, we're good," Colt says seriously. "That woman is four for four with matchmaking. I don't want to end up on her hit list."

GG is known for her, ah, tarot card abilities. I'll admit, it's a little nerve racking.

"That's right, Colt. Come on, Conflicted Heart, we have to be up bright and early, ya know. I can't be late for readin' my cards." Everyone gasps as GG enters the room. We all stare, wide-eyed.

Who the hell is she talking about now?

When she stops in front of me, everyone else in the room smirks. She only gives nicknames to those she's ready to match up. All four of her last marks are now married, or soon to be married. I can't control the shiver that runs down my spine.

"Looks like Seth is on the chopping block next," Colton laughs.

"Thank God it isn't me," Halton grumbles. "It's late. I'm going to bed. We can make a plan in the morning. Get me all your financials, and I'll start first thing." With that, he heads out of the run-down lodge for his room.

Staring up at GG, I realize she definitely has me in her sights, and it scares the shit out of me. I'm a widower, and I'm not ready to move on, but GG is a scary magician. I have a feeling whatever comes next will test everything I know to be true.

~

I meet GG in the lodge at six a.m. the next morning, and she explains that the general store isn't open yet, but she gets there early to set up.

What am I supposed to do for two hours until the shop opens?

"Just be friendly, Conflicted. People around here are lookin' for real, honest folk. Do that, and you'll be just fine."

Peering over at GG in the passenger seat, I'm amazed by how easily she has accepted all the new people in her life. Her other granddaughter, Lanie, married another Westbrook adoptee, Dexter.

"I'll try. I haven't been too social the last few years," I admit.

She shocks the hell out of me when she rests her hand on mine and squeezes. "Losin' one love of your life doesn't mean you stop livin', son. There's a lot of good left to be had, trust me. When my Benny died, a piece of me got buried right alongside him. But, I was an old bird by then. You may be missing a piece of yourself, but you've got a full life ahead of ya. Don't forget that. Sometimes a little heartbreak makes loving someone that much more meaningful."

I don't say anything as I pull into the store's parking lot. Her words hang heavy in the silence. When I park, I help her pull out her supplies and carry them to the front door, which opens with ease even at the early hour.

I'm shocked to see the place packed already.

"I thought they didn't open for two hours," I whisper to GG.

With a wink, she cackles, "Those hours are for tourists, Conflicted. You're one of us now."

Involuntarily, I roll my eyes. If one more family claims me, I'm not sure what I'll do with myself, but I dutifully follow GG anyway.

After placing her box on the folding table, I turn to grab more supplies when I collide with someone, nearly knocking her to the ground. Wrapping my arms around her middle just before she hits the ground, she brushes her wispy, dark hair out of her eyes, and I'm caught in her spell.

"Are … are you okay?" I finally choke out, not realizing I'm still holding her precariously above the floor.

Her eyes are as blue as the Caribbean and cartoonishly wide. "I-I-I'm fine."

"Jesus, I'm so sorry."

"All right there, Conflicted. How about you let Disheartened up, huh?"

I heard GG, but the woman in my arms holds my gaze captive, like time is standing still. It isn't until she wiggles, trying to stand, that I realize what GG just said. She gave this girl a nickname.

"Sorry," I mutter, helping her to her feet. "Ah, I'm Seth."

Flustered, she smooths out her shirt as an older man walks up behind her.

"Are you a Westbrook or a Macomb?" she asks, her tone icy.

Well, shit.

Pinching the back of my neck, I peer down at her. Technically, I'm neither. I'm a Foster, but since the Westbrooks have adopted me into their fold, I guess you could lump me in with them. After a moment, I answer evasively, "I've never met a Macomb."

The beautiful girl in front of me narrows her eyes.

"Ari, are you okay?" the older man asks. When she nods, he turns his attention to me. "Are you here with the Westbrooks?"

Ari.

"Now, John, he's with me. Whatever you wanna call him, he's on our side," GG informs the room that has now taken an interest in me.

I can't take my eyes off of Ari. I'm stuck in her vortex, and I can't get out.

GG stares between the two of us and smirks. "Yup, I think this will be my easiest match yet."

We both whip our gazes to her. My fingers can still feel Ari's soft skin beneath them, and shockingly, I'm itching to touch her again. I take half a step forward before I realize what I'm doing.

"GG, *this* is who you think my match is?" Ari's sweet voice is at war with her words.

"No, girly. I know it is."

I gape between the two. I'm shocked that the world around GG just accepts her card reading as gospel and that I'm having such a bizarre reaction to a girl who is clearly too young for me.

"GG, I think you're mixed up with this one," I begin.

"Why's that? Is my Ari not good enough for you?" The man GG called John bullies himself to the front of the line.

"Ah, no, sir. I just meant ... Ah." I can feel my face flaming. "I just meant that I'm too old for her."

"Tsk, tsk," GG remarks.

"What's going on in here?" a voice so shrill it could cut glass calls out from the back of the shop.

Following the sound, I see two frumpy girls closer to my age making their way toward us.

"Shit," Ari whispers.

Turning my attention back to her, I notice her posture stiffening the closer these dingbats get to us, and I don't like it.

"Yup, here comes the show," GG exclaims.

"Ari, why are you just standing around? Don't you have work to do?" one of the snarky girls asks. Resting bitch face has never been more pronounced.

Feeling as though I need to stick up for a girl I don't even know, I take a step forward. "Actually, it's my fault. I ran into her and nearly knocked her over. I'm just making sure she's okay."

I see the moment these girls sense fresh meat and internally cringe.

"Oh, I'm sure it was all her fault. It always is. Isn't that right, Ariana?" The catty cow's words drip with contempt, and I take a step toward my new obsession. My subconscious gets whiplash as my thoughts go haywire.

"Tiffany, did you need something?" Ari asks, exasperated, but I'm surprised by her meek tone.

Who the hell are these girls?

"Well," the other one starts, "there are no eggs or bread upstairs. How are we supposed to get ready for our busy day without breakfast?"

"Brittany, you're twenty-eight years old. If you can't figure out how to make it down the stairs to get our own damn groceries, you're dumber than I thought," John remarks.

"Uncle Baker, that won't help," Ari whispers.

As if pulled by a string, he and I both take a step toward Ari. In an unspoken move, we buffer her on either side from the twatwaffles in front of us.

One of the girls, Tiffany, I think, scowls as I stand guard at Ari's side. She takes a step closer to me, and I'm overwhelmed by the scent of cheap perfume. "Tell me, handsome, are you a Westbrook or a Macomb?"

What the hell is with this town?

"Listen, sponge, Seth is with me. He isn't interested in being your sugar daddy," GG states matter-of-factly.

"Sponge?" she asks, confused.

GG smiles. "Would you prefer gold digger?"

"Okay, guys, that's enough. Tiffany? Brittany? Why don't you go upstairs and get ready for your spa day? I'll bring up some breakfast as soon as I get everyone settled down here."

Tiffany inches closer and runs her finger down my chest. "I'd rather have him for breakfast."

The gagging noise that erupts from my throat is involuntary, but it makes her take a step back.

"What? Don't you want someone to show you around town, handsome?" Her attempt at sounding seductive makes my stomach turn.

"Actually, I already have one. I'm looking forward to spending time alone with Ri here." I don't know what caused me to say that, but as soon as it's out of my mouth, I know it's true.

CHAPTER 4

ARI

What the hell is happening? What does he mean he's looking forward to spending time alone with me? I haven't even spoken a complete sentence to him in the ten minutes he's been in my store.

"Yes," Uncle Baker speaks up. "I was just telling Mr. Seth here that I would fill in for Ari today so she could finally have a break and maybe get an actual meal in her belly," he says, staring pointedly at Seth.

"What the heck? Uncle Baker, what are you talking about?"

"She can't just take the day off," Brittany protests. I'm half expecting to see a foot stomp, too. "She has to run the store."

"I worked in this shop with her father for years before you brats moved in. I can handle it for a day." His arctic tone does nothing to call off my tormentors.

I chance a peek at Seth and see he's volleying back and forth, trying to follow the argument happening all around us. *Ugh, how can he look so sexy even wearing a look of confusion?*

"And I worked here before that," GG chimes in. "John and I have this shop under control."

"Are you sure I can trust my baby girl with that man?" I hear uncle Baker whisper to GG.

"That *man* helped save my Lexi girl and brought her home to me. I know you can trust him," GG shoots back.

"Wait, everyone, just wait. What are you talking about?"

Seth is looking a little green, and I can't say I blame him.

"Nothing, dear. Come on, Ari, let's grab your coat." Uncle Baker hurries me to the back of the shop. "Get a move on, girly, before the wicked stepmother gets down here. And, don't you say a word, GG and I can handle that old bitty, so don't you worry about a thing. Take Seth out and show him around. We're on a time crunch here to get the town to fall in love with all the Westbrooks, so don't be shy about introducing him to people."

"But, I—"

"No buts. Here, slip this on." He's sliding my arms into a coat before my brain has had a second to catch up.

"Are you seriously sending me out for the day with some random stranger?"

"He's not a stranger. His name is Seth, and GG vouched for him. He's as good as family," Uncle Baker says smoothly.

Before I can think of a rebuttal, he ushers me to the front of the store where Brittany and Tiffany stand, gaping.

"Hey, that's my new jacket. You can't wear it. You'll stretch it all out," Tiffany whines, which is funny since she's twice my size. Before I make it to the door, she rips it off me, then screams about me ruining it.

I stare open-mouthed at the chaos happening all around when I hear Virginia's voice yelling down the stairs, and I hang my head in defeat.

"Conflicted? Get Dissy out of here, now, and show her a good day," GG scolds, snapping us all out of our stupor.

"Dissy?"

"I can't go around yelling Disheartened all the time, now

can I? Get going." GG makes a shooing motion toward the door.

I'm so embarrassed, and poor Seth looks horrified as he guides me out the door. We walk at a brisk pace to his truck, where he opens the door, and I slide in. I wish these plush, leather seats would swallow me whole as I watch him round the hood and climb in next to me.

He stares straight ahead for a moment before starting the ignition.

"What the hell just happened?" he finally asks.

I drop my head into my hands, trying not to cry. "I'm so sorry, Seth ... for everything. If you could just drop me off around the corner, I'll find a place to hide out for a few hours, so you don't catch shit from GG."

"Ari?" He says it so gently, I'm compelled to meet his gaze. "Why would I do that? I would very much like to spend the day with you. I do need a tour guide, and it seems like you could use a break, am I right?" The smile that overtakes his handsome face shows off perfectly straight, white teeth.

His dark brown hair is high and tight, making me think of the army. I heard GG say he saved Lexi last year, so that would make sense. I know I'm staring, but it's his kind eyes, the darkest shade of navy, that reel me in.

"A-Are you sure? I know you got roped into spending time with me. You probably have a million other things you could be doing."

He places an enormous hand carefully on my forearm. "Ri, I always say what I mean. Always. I would love to hang out with you today. Apparently, I'm the new face of The Westbrook Group, at least for Burke Hollow, so maybe you can give me the lay of the land."

When he winks, my stomach does a strange little dance. The heat of his hand goes straight to my core, and I shift uncomfortably. In all of my twenty-four years, I've never had this kind of reaction to a man.

"Shit, are you cold? What the hell happened in there, and why did crazy lady number one rip that jacket off you?"

"It wasn't my jacket … it was hers. I was so confused by everything happening that I didn't realize Uncle Baker had put it on me."

"Whatever, Ri, that's not a normal reaction. Who are those girls? They treated you like shit."

Hearing him call me Ri causes the flutter in my tummy again. *My lady bits need an ice bath.*

"It's a really long story, but they're my stepsisters."

"Well, I hope you'll tell me about it someday. But, seriously, they take evil stepsisters to a whole other level," he jokes while backing the truck out of his parking spot. "Er, don't tell me there's an evil stepmother, too?"

I follow his line of sight to see Virginia standing in the doorway, scowling and waving wildly.

"Shit." I breathe heavily and start to unbuckle. "I'd better go back in there. If I don't work at the store today, she'll just make tomorrow miserable for me."

I'm shocked when Seth's finger finds its way to my chin and lifts my face to meet his. "Is this what your life is like every day?"

"It wasn't always like this," I say, feeling the need to defend my father. "I was happy once. My mother and father were amazing. When my mom got sick, a little piece of my father died, too. He didn't know how to care for me as I got older, so he remarried, thinking it would be good for me to have a woman around. We had no idea what Virginia was like until it was too late. Then, my dad had a heart attack, and she took over."

Peering up, I see her stomping through the parking lot, screaming something I can't hear. Seth glances from her to me, pushes my buckle back into the slot, then shifts the car into drive and speeds off.

"Fuck that, Ri. I'll help you deal with the fallout tomorrow, but if you have to live with that bullshit day in and day out, I'm taking you for some fun today. Show me the ropes—where's our first stop?"

I nibble my bottom lip. It's early summer in Vermont, which means it is still a little chilly, so what better way to ingratiate him to our culture than by taking him to Eggy's Grille.

"Have you eaten yet?" I feel a smile make its way across my face.

"No. GG said we'd eat at the store."

"Then take Route 15 for two miles. You're about to meet the whole town at once."

To his credit, he doesn't complain, even if his body language indicates he's not comfortable. The bulging muscle of his forearm as he grips the steering wheel is a dead giveaway.

"Done," he finally sighs. He glances in my direction a few times before asking, "Ri? How old are you?"

I stare at him for a moment, trying to gauge his age. I can tell he's older than me, and the scars on his hands point to a harder life than mine, but behind his scowl, I see a young man. He can't be that much older.

"I'm twenty-four. How old are you?"

"Shit," he groans, and I position myself in the seat so I can watch him. He makes eye contact briefly, and I swear he just obliterated my panties.

No, Ari, stop it. This is simply a newcomer needing a tour guide, nothing more. *Yeah, right. Someone tell that to my ovaries.*

"Ah, I'm old," he says evasively.

I simply stare, waiting for an actual answer, and he finally relents.

"I'm thirty-two."

So eight years older than me. Daddy was ten years older than Mom. It can work. *Geez, Ari, what the hell are you think-*

ing? I've known this guy for all of five minutes. I don't know if it's my silence or something else, but Seth starts rambling like a nervous teenager on prom night.

"I'm a widower. I have a six-year-old little girl named Sadie, who's my entire world. I spent my adult life in a secret branch of the US military. Now, two of my buddies and I have purchased a security company, except I'm not really sure how it's going to work yet. On our last mission, we were held captive. Ashton, he's the one who works behind the scenes, was injured pretty badly. He's in a dark place, and I don't know what will pull him out of it. Until then, I'm kind of in limbo, except where my daughter is concerned. She always comes first. My wife died two years ago. I haven't been on a date or had sex since then."

I sit back, stunned.

"Oh, my God, I'm so sorry," he blurts, still on a roll. "I-I don't know what the hell just came over me. I never spew personal shit like that, not ever. Not since Reb …" He drifts off, lost in thought.

"Not since your wife?" I supply. I don't know why I push this, it's none of my business, but I feel connected to him.

"Yeah," he answers quietly. "Not since Rebecca."

"Would it help if I told you some of my story?"

He chuckles. "Thank you for trying to make me feel better, but that's not necessary. Not unless you want to, I mean."

He's getting more awkward by the minute, and it makes me want to push him a little more.

"Well, my dad died three years ago while I was in art school. My mother was an artist, and she was amazing. When my dad passed away, I had to come home to run the store because Virginia refused to pay my tuition, and it was too late to apply for loans. She pays me less than minimum wage for about half of the hours I actually work.

"About six months ago, I went upstairs after closing the

store to find all my stuff in the hallway. She had moved me out of my childhood room so her daughter could have it. There are only three bedrooms, and she said I wasn't allowed to sleep on the couch, so I moved to the shed out back. It's not as bad as it sounds, though," I add quickly. "My dad had used it as a man cave for years. Now I know why he needed an escape." I chuckle, but there's no humor in it.

"A week later, I found out they painted over the murals my mother had done in my room. The store is my dad's legacy. The building is the last connection I have to my mom, so I'm stuck because Vermont law says Virginia got it all when my dad passed away."

Seth pulls off to the side of the road. Glancing around, I realize we are already at the town square.

"That's really fucked up, Ri. I'm sorry."

"Life isn't all fairytales and happy endings, Seth. It is what it is."

CHAPTER 5

SETH

We sit in the cab of the truck, just staring at each other for a few minutes. The silence isn't uncomfortable, though. In fact, I'm more at ease with Ari than I am with the Westbrooks, and that scares the living shit out of me.

"So, this is actually a great place to park. We can walk from here, and the second the town's people get word there's a new face, the sidewalks will fill pretty quickly. Just …" She trails off and searches my face again. "Maybe try to tone down the scowl?"

I scoff, offended. "I'm not scowling."

Ari reaches up and runs her forefinger along the crease between my eyebrows. *When the hell did that happen?*

"For someone that isn't scowling, these scrunched-up eyebrows tell a different story. You look kind of scary. Not that it isn't sexy and all, but you actually want people to talk to you, right? You're the spokesman for The Westbrook Group?"

Climbing out of the truck, I raise and lower my eyebrows a few times, attempting to relax them when a thought occurs.

Ari thinks I'm sexy. Four little words have my face calming as a genuine smile forms.

"Good! Whatever you're thinking about, keep it up. You almost look friendly," she teases as she approaches me on the sidewalk.

Leaning in, I lower my voice, and it takes on a gravel-like quality. "Do you want to know what I'm thinking about, Ri?"

"Ah ... er, prob-probably n-not," she stammers, taking half a step back, but I move in tandem.

"Are you sure?" I wiggle my eyebrows, and I see her neck working to swallow.

"Why do I have the feeling it's something dirty?"

My bark of laughter is unexpected and catches us both off guard. The thing is, I am. I'm thinking very dirty thoughts about this girl, and my mind is raging a battle I can't win. There's no denying I'm attracted to her, but I made a vow to Rebecca. I'm not sure I'm ready to let go of that yet.

"Miss Winters? May I have a word with you?"

Turning my head, I see an older man with a cane heading our way, and if I have a scowl, he has perfected the glower. I'm willing to bet his is permanent, though, and I make a conscious decision to work on my eyebrows from now on.

"Here's your first test," Ari whispers under her breath.

"Mr. Fontaine, how nice to see you again."

The harrumph that comes out of his mouth is all the greeting she gets in return.

"Who is this man?"

I can't tell yet if he is anti-Westbrook or Macomb, but whoever it is, it will take a miracle to win him over.

"This is Seth. Seth, ah ..."

"Seth Foster, sir. It's nice to meet you." I hold out my hand to shake while giving Ari a shit-eating grin.

Mr. Fontaine stares at my hand with unadulterated disgust.

"What side is he on?"

He directs it to Ari, but I've already had enough of his bullshit.

"I'm an honorary Westbrook if that is what you're asking."

"Great," he grumbles. "Just what I need."

"I'm sorry? Is there something I can help you with?" I struggle to keep my tone even until I hear Ari's voice in my head. *"It's sexy and all."* Suddenly, working to stay neutral isn't all that hard anymore.

"I doubt it. We need jobs in this town. Jobs Macomb will bring. You Westbrooks haven't promised us anything."

Damn it, Easton. Why the hell didn't he prepare me for an ambush? Glancing around, I see a crowd is gathering, just as Ari predicted.

"Well, sir, I just got into town late last night, but I'm sure …"

The door behind me swings open, and I glance up at the sign. Hattie's Happy Hardware Haven. *What the hell kind of name is that?* When I see someone approach, I shift to let the newcomer enter the circle that has gathered while I get my thoughts in order. Luckily, it turns out I don't have to. Easton now stands beside me with a trolley behind him, full of building materials.

"Fontaine," East says in greeting. I can tell by his posture he isn't pleased to see him. "I see you've met my good friend, Seth. He's here to help us get our proposal in order. I couldn't help but overhear your questions, and perhaps I'm better suited to answer them until Seth has had time to properly acclimate to the area? What is it I can do for you?"

He's perfectly polite, but there's no mistaking the tension radiating off every muscle. *What could he possibly have against this eighty-year-old man?*

"I said, Macomb will bring jobs to town, and you've made no effort to communicate your offer to anyone here."

"That's true. I've been busting my ass repairing GG's lodge, but that doesn't mean we have nothing to offer. We're still working out details, but I assure you that our offer will be truly in the best interests of this town and its people. I'm not interested in handing over a onetime lump sum. I want to invigorate the town so it can prosper on its own. The Westbrook Group is a billion-dollar conglomerate, so moving pieces take time. I am in no way hiding anything from you. Now, Seth? Why don't you and Ari continue with your day?" He turns back to Mr. Fontaine. "I have to get back to the lodge. If you have questions, I strongly suggest you find me," Easton growls, and Mr. Fontaine takes a shaky step back.

What is going on?

"Seth, I'll see you back at GG's place." East doesn't wait for a reply. Instead, he parts the crowd and begins loading up his supplies into the back of a beat-up, old Ford.

"Come on, let's go talk to Abe and Hattie." Ari pulls on my sleeve, and I finally tear my gaze away from East.

"Yeah, okay. I hope it won't be as fucked up as that interaction was."

"Well," she draws out, "it'll be interesting for sure, but in a haha kind of way. I think."

My eyes roll to the back of my head, and I let out a sigh. This is going to be a long-ass day.

~

Three hours later, I've met Abe and Hattie Laroe. They own Hattie's Happy Hardware Haven, and now I understand the name. Dressed in hemp and smelling of patchouli, they're modern day hippies.

Then we met GG's partner in crime, Betty Anne, and I was immediately put on some massive text chain that everyone in town gets. By the time I left her, my phone was blowing up with messages about the handsome new hottie in town. I was getting texts about myself, and I could do nothing but shake my head.

Our last stop was the one gas station in town called Toots. Apparently, it also serves as a pizza shop.

"Did you know Garret Wiley, the owner of Toots, was Lexi's high school sweetheart?"

"Really?" He was nice enough, but not someone I could picture with Lexi. And, I'm willing to bet Easton hates him.

We're sitting in the gazebo at the town square having a late lunch with sandwiches that GG drove into town.

"I feel like I've found myself in the twilight zone or something," I admit.

"This town has a way of doing that." Ari smiles, and a familiar but long buried ache spreads throughout my chest. Her dark hair is styled in a pixie cut that frames her face, accenting large, expressive eyes, and I feel myself getting lost in her again.

"Do you—"

I'm interrupted when the speakers above us crackle to life. Ed Sheeran's "Perfect" drifts down.

"What's this?" I ask, but Ari appears as confused as I am.

"Ask her to dance," GG's voice rings loud. Way too loud. Glancing around, I find her and Betty Anne hunched together behind the bushes, laughing like schoolgirls.

"Are they serious?"

Hanging my head, I laugh. "I've seen GG in action a couple of times now. She doesn't give up. It's probably best if we just follow orders."

I hold my hand out to Ari, and she reluctantly slips her delicate fingers into my palm.

Her heat travels throughout my body like your first shot of whiskey. It warms me from the inside out, leaving a contended feeling in its wake.

I think I might be well and truly fucked.

I pull until she's standing and slowly tug her toward me.

"Ask her, you big lug." This time it's Betty Anne's voice that comes over the megaphone.

Glancing over my shoulder, I see Betty Anne's blue tinted white hair peeking out over the top of a hydrangea bush.

Ari giggles, and I follow suit.

"They're relentless. Would you like to dance, Ri?"

"I guess we'd better."

Clutching my chest with my free hand, I feign heartache. "Ouch ... you wound me, woman."

"Something tells me your ego is just fine."

Ari is playful and light. Something that hasn't been a part of my life for a long time. The only exception is Sadie; she brings sunshine wherever she goes. Ari is different, and I can't quite place what it is. Yes, I'm attracted to her, but it's the connection I feel that unnerves me.

"You're right, but that doesn't mean you can't play along." I smirk, pulling her body into mine.

The second I wrap my arms around her waist, she inhales deeply, as if I shocked her.

"We have to be close to dance, sweetheart."

She nods frantically but doesn't speak. Slowly, our bodies meld into one, and we sway in time with the music. Ari rests her head on my chest, and the sensation brands me. I haven't had a woman in my arms in a long time, and I've never had a visceral reaction as I am to Ari. I know I'm going to have to work out what that means, but I'm selfish and revel in the contact for now.

The song winds down, and I prepare to part, but it loops and starts again. I turn us to face GG, who smirks behind her bush.

"Does she seriously think we can't see her?" Ari asks.

"The only thing I know about GG is not to question her," I sigh.

Ari gives in and rests her head back on my chest. The friction of our bodies is wreaking havoc on my manhood, and I pray to God that she can't feel my erection. I don't remember the last time I sported a boner in broad daylight, but it's becoming painful. The scent of her jasmine shampoo drifts to my nose, and I lower my head to inhale her. If I'm not careful, this girl could quickly become my addiction.

"Kiss her," comes a voice through the megaphone I don't recognize.

"Uncle Baker," Ari hisses. "You're supposed to be running the store."

Oh shit. I know she's worried about that place. If both GG and Baker are here, what does that mean for her shop?

"Don't get ya panties in a twist there, Dissy. We're out to lunch. We'll open back up within the hour," GG scolds.

"Kiss her. Kiss her. Kiss her," Baker chants.

"I can't believe this," Ari cries, and buries her face in my shirt. "So freaking embarrassing."

Looping my fingers under her chin, I lift her face and see it in her eyes. She wants me to kiss her as much as I need to do it. We gaze at each other for long moments before I work up the courage to speak.

"If we give them what they want, we have a better chance of getting them to leave," I reason.

Ari swallows a few times, never taking her eyes off mine, and then gives an almost imperceptible nod.

"Can I kiss you, sweet Ri?"

"Y-Yes." Her voice is quiet and uncertain, but there will be nothing uncertain about this kiss.

With her permission, I cradle her face in my hands. Then, with eyes wide open, I slowly lower my lips to hers.

CHAPTER 6

ARI

Holy hell, this man can kiss! He's sweet and gentle at first, making me think that's how he'll keep it. But two seconds after our lips touch, a growl erupts from deep in his throat, and I gasp. As soon as my lips separate, he plunges his tongue into the depths of my mouth.

I've never been kissed like this in my life. His tongue wars with mine for control, and I finally concede. He works my tongue and lips as if they're a part of him. I attempt to recognize what he tastes like, but my brain cells shoot off rockets in my head like the Fourth of July. I'm lost. Completely and totally lost to this stranger.

Seth's hand snakes down my back, and he hauls me even closer to him. I gasp as I feel his enormous length pressing against my belly, and that breaks our spell. He lingers with a few small, chaste pecks to my lips, then slowly pulls away.

Resting his forehead on mine, he lets out a ragged breath. "Holy shit."

Attempting to return my heart rate to normal, I laugh. "Yeah, holy shit about sums that up. I-I didn't know kisses could do that."

Even with our foreheads still touching, I can see him smirk.

"Do what exactly?" His voice is strangled, and it's encouraging to know I'm not alone in what I'm feeling.

"Make me feel alive? Make me forget my name? Make me want to do it again?" Instantly, I squeeze my eyes shut tight and feel my nose wrinkle. I cannot believe I just said all that out loud. "Make me spew embarrassing things that should stay in my head?" I whisper.

Seth chuckles, and I feel it everywhere. Even his laugh is freaking sexy.

"Phase one complete. As you were, kids," GG's voice echoes through the megaphone.

"I've never experienced this level of crazy, and I was a secret agent," Seth admits.

"Welcome to Burke Hollow." I shrug and reluctantly pull away.

"So far, I've been welcomed to the chaos and welcomed to Burke Hollow. Both have been full of surprises."

I can't tell from his tone if that's a good thing or not, and I'm already too invested not to ask.

"Good surprises, or bad?" There's a vulnerability in my voice that I need to get a handle on before I drop to the ground and beg him to take me. *Where in the hell are these thoughts coming from? Seriously, Ari. Get your shit together, girl!*

Reaching for me, he takes my hand in his. After glancing over his shoulder to make sure the peanut gallery has moved on, he lowers his voice. "All good, Ari. Confusing and scary, but good. I think."

He thinks? Great. Thanks for that.

"What's the frown for?" he asks softly.

"I'm not frowning. What do you mean?"

"You look as though I just kicked your puppy, Ri. What's the face for?"

"Nothing. I'm happy you *think* everything's been mostly good. I mean, that's great, right?"

"Ah-huh." He pauses while his eyes squint, assessing me. "Listen, maybe we should clear up a few things."

Is this where he gives me the brush off? After that freaking kiss? Is he serious?

"Nothing to clear up, Seth. We're good. Anywhere else you want to see today? Or should we head back?"

He stands in front of me with his arms crossed over his chest. Seth's scary when he's like this, and I can totally see how he would be a kick ass spy, but if he thinks he can kiss the hell out of me in one breath and send me packing on the next, he has another thing coming. For show or not, that was not the brush-off kind of kiss. Even I know that.

"What are you doing tonight?" he asks, catching me off guard.

"Ah." I glance at my watch, then all around us to see if GG and Uncle Baker have somehow put him up to another charade. When I know that we're all alone, I force my brain to work. "I'm just, ah, getting the shop ready for the morning rush, I guess."

"Not anymore. Lexi is insisting we go to a place called the Packing House tonight. We'll pick you up on the way."

Now it's my turn to stand indignantly. "With you?"

"Yeah."

"To the Packing House?"

He raises his eyebrows like he's trying really hard not to lose his shit. "That's what I said, Ri."

"Like, on a date?"

This causes him to sputter, and before he can respond, embarrassment takes over.

"Never mind, Seth. I'm just messing with you." Turning, I head back to our seats to pack up the remnants of our lunch.

"I'm really fucking this all up, aren't I?"

I can hear the conflict in his voice, and I don't want to be the cause of it. I'm already settling for so much in my life. I won't allow romance to be one of them.

"Nah, it was a good day, Seth. Everyone in town loves you, for the most part anyway. I'd say it was a success, no?"

He walks forward, never taking his eyes off me. "It was the best day, Ri. But I'm talking about this, right here. You and me."

My voice chooses this exact moment to freeze up.

Placing his hands on my shoulders, he lowers his gaze until I'm forced to look at him. "I don't know how to do this, Ri. Any of this." He sighs and pulls away. "I was a teenager when I met Rebecca. I don't even think I ever really asked her out on a date. So, I don't know how to do any of this." He gestures between the two of us.

"I-I'm not really sure what you're saying, Seth."

"Come out with us tonight? With me? Come out with me? I'm only here for a week, but I like you. I like spending time with you. I've never had many friends, and the ones that I do have I either know through SIA or, strangely, they've adopted me."

Friend? He wants to be friends after that kiss? I mean, I guess it makes sense. He's only here for a week, and truth be told, I don't have any friends. *Friends?* Gah, it sounds bitter even in my head, but a friend is better than nothing at this point. Plus, if I'm already going to deal with hell tomorrow for skipping out on the store today, I might as well have fun tonight.

"Sure. I don't really have many friends either, so it might be fun."

Seth winces, and I wonder if I said something wrong.

"Great. Friends, tonight, with the Westbrooks. It'll be, ah, it'll be fun."

Now it's my turn to stare at him. I have a distinct impression that I'm missing something.

"Awesome," it comes out forced. "So, should we head

back? I think you've met pretty much everyone in town by now."

He pinches the back of his neck, then rolls his shoulders before responding. "Sure, Ri. Let's head back. I'll drop you off so we can all get ready. I'll check with Lexi when I get back to the lodge and let you know what time we'll pick you up."

After I toss our trash in the barrel, I turn to find Seth staring at me. A mix of emotions I can't begin to understand cloud his face.

"Sure, sounds good. GG will have my number at the lodge."

We walk back to his truck in silence. I feel him watching me, but I'm drained right now. I just need to get home and think about all the crazy shit running through my head.

Less than fifteen minutes later, he's walking me to my door. I'm not ashamed of where I live, but I'm not exactly ready for houseguests either, so I say good-bye and slip through the door before he can really get a look inside.

I can hear him pacing on the other side of the door, and I feel guilty. I don't know what I feel guilty for, exactly, but the fact that he seems so conflicted doesn't sit right with me.

Eventually, I hear the gravel move under his feet as he walks back to his truck, and I slide down the wall. Sitting on the floor, I stare at the ceiling. How the hell has my life come to this? Better yet, why has it taken a stranger barging into my world for me to see it?

CHAPTER 7

SETH

It was just a kiss. A simple kiss with an audience. A goddamn kiss that has my hands shaking as I drive back up the mountain.

Maybe I'm just hard up? Hand jobs in the shower won't cut it forever, I know that, but that fucking kiss? I hate myself right now because my brain keeps trying to compare it to Rebecca. I love my wife; I always have. She was the love of my life.

But she's not here anymore, Seth.

I pull up to the lodge and can't get the truck into park fast enough. I'm suffocating in here. As soon as I turn off the ignition, I'm jumping outside, breathing too heavily to calm down. *What the hell is happening to me?* I undo the top few buttons on my shirt, thinking it will help. It doesn't.

"You okay?"

Spinning in place, I notice Lexi sitting on the porch with a drink I hope contains vodka.

"I-I don't know, Lex. It's been a pretty fucked up day."

"Welcome to my world," she says sadly. Holding up a bottle of Tito's, she shakes an empty glass in my direction. "Wanna drink?"

I'm not much a drinker, mainly because I spent my life in the military where I could be called to duty at any time, but I need that damn drink right now.

"Yes, Jesus, make it strong."

"GG said you made a match today?" She smirks.

I give her the side-eye. "Were you out here waiting for me?"

Lexi shrugs, and her blonde hair falls behind her shoulder.

"Maybe. I love this town, but I know it can be a lot. I also know the Westbrooks can be overwhelming when they're trying to do good."

I know Lexi doesn't share her personal shit—it's one of the reasons we get along so well—but I'd be an asshole if I didn't at least try to be there for her, too.

"Easton has been here a long time. Any reason for that?"

"He's a stubborn, arrogant, bos—"

"Helper. A strong, opinionated helper are the words you're looking for, Locket."

Locket? There's definitely something going on between these two.

"Lexi," she hisses, glancing around uncomfortably. "We're talking about Seth, anyway."

"What about him?" East asks, joining us on the wraparound porch. I don't miss that he walks past multiple empty seats to sit down right beside Lexi. You couldn't fit a piece of paper between them right now, and she's flushing red.

"We're talking about why he looks like he's trying to jump out of his skin."

"What? No, we aren't. You asked if I wanted a drink," I remind her.

"Because you were two seconds away from tearing your shirt to shreds when you couldn't get your buttons undone in time."

Knowing she's right, I lean back into the oversized

Adirondack chair and take a long sip of whatever Lexi just handed me.

"So, what has your panties in a twist?" Easton asks, leaning back into his chair. The movement forces Lexi to lean into him.

"Ari Winters." Even saying her name causes my soul to split in two. Half of me is one spark away from igniting feelings, and the other half is berating me for cheating on Rebecca.

"You like her," Lexi states with a half-smile.

"I made a vow a long time ago to Rebecca."

Easton takes the glass from Lexi's hand and chugs half her drink before speaking. "Listen, Seth. I commend you for keeping your vow, I do. I know that pain. I've lived it. The difference is, Rebecca loved you with everything she had." He runs a hand through his hair roughly before continuing. "Loki's told me a little about her. I know you had an epic love story, and nothing will ever take that away, but that kind of love you had for each other? That's the kind of love that needs to carry on. Rebecca would have wanted you to live your life. Loving someone else doesn't take away from the love you had for her."

"Whoa. Seriously? I've known Ari for all of ten hours. I'm not saying there isn't a possibility of more, but love, East? I think you've been watching too many Hallmark movies."

"Right?" Lexi gasps, still attempting to scoot away from Easton, who's holding her shoulder tight, keeping her in place. "Insta love never works out. It's not real. Insta lust? Maybe. But not love."

"That's bullshit, and you know it, Lex." Easton's voice is firm but full of emotion.

"What's going on between the two of you?" I finally ask.

"Nothing," Lexi forces out.

"Life," Easton says at the same time.

"Seth, listen. If you like this girl, don't let her get away.

Figure out what's holding you back and knock it down. Life is too short not to experience love in all its forms. Do whatever you need to do to move on, then lock it down before it's too late."

I stare at Easton, who rarely speaks more than a few muttered words at a time. I'm shocked by his vehemence, but watching him with Lexi, I realize he's speaking his truth.

"How does Ari feel? Did you ever stop to consider she may not want anything to do with him? Maybe she's just perfectly happy to be on her own where nothing can hurt her. Sometimes living means surviving, and sometimes, that means relying only on yourself."

I slink back into my seat. They're definitely not talking about Ari and me anymore.

"We're not meant to be solitary creatures, Locket." Easton's raised voice causes her to flinch. "You're lying to yourself if you think you don't need love. That you don't crave it. That you don't deserve it. Not everyone in this world is out to get you. Not everyone will hurt you."

Lexi bolts upright and wraps her arms around herself as if she's trying to disappear. "We're not talking about me, Beast. None of this is about me, or you, or us. There is no us. There will not be an us. You need to know that we would never work. I'm not what you need," she screams. In the same breath, she realizes they have an audience. Flustered, she grabs her drink and stomps down the stairs, just as GG pulls up the long drive.

Lexi hops off the steps toward her grandmother but yells over her shoulder, "Seth? Pick me up at Ari's on the way to the Packing House."

"What? You know her?"

"Not really. She's a few years younger than me, but this is Burke Hollow," she calls without looking back. "We'll be best friends by sundown."

"Ah, what the hell are you doing then?"

"I'm going to vet your new girl. You've got to have quite the backbone to survive the chaos we've found ourselves in." She smiles, but it seems forced.

"You can't do that, Lex. You don't even know her? What are you going to do, just barge into her house? They have her living in some she-shed, anyway. I'm not sure she wants visitors."

She slams the door of GG's truck, then rolls down the window. "The Westbrooks have their chaos; Burke Hollow has their own. It'll be fine, Seth. Just don't be late picking me up."

"I'm fucking driving, Locket," East growls, and I watch idiotically as GG backs out of the driveway.

"What just happened?"

"Lexi is the master of goddamn avoidance, that's what happened."

Turning in my seat, I study Easton. He looks tired and sad.

"What—"

He holds up a hand to cut me off. "I don't have any answers for you, Seth. I think I'm losing my fucking mind. I'll tell you, though, if you like this girl, don't let anything keep you from her."

"I'm confused," I finally admit. "I love Rebecca. I have Sadie to think about. Ari freaking lives in Vermont. I haven't even spared another woman a second glance in almost ten years, then Ari comes along and obliterates my perfectly simple life with one insane kiss."

"Hold up. You kissed her?"

"Ugh," I groan. "I was kind of tricked into it. Or strong-armed. GG showed up in the park with music and a megaphone."

Easton doubles over, cradling his belly as he laughs. "Only in this town, and only GG. How was it?"

"The kiss or the meddling?"

Easton raises his eyebrows.

"The kiss was soul-crushingly amazing. The meddling, not so much."

"Well, you're here for a week without Sadie, right? Seems like the perfect time to figure out what you want."

"What about you?"

The sardonic laugh that erupts from deep in Easton's throat gives away his frustration. "I know what I want, Seth. But grief is a dark and fucked up emotion. I'm starting to think that no matter how much I try, I'll never pull her from it."

I know Lexi's been through a lot, but the sadness Easton expresses on her behalf sits heavy in my chest.

"Are you happy, East?"

"I'm getting there. It's just a lot more fucking work than I ever imagined. Find your happy, man. Find it and hold on for dear life. There's a lot of fucked up in this world. If you find someone who can make you see the light through all that darkness? Let yourself have it. Allow yourself that one grace."

"You know, for a grumpy bastard, you've got a lot of flowery things to say lately."

He stares at the road Lexi just left on. "There's nothing flowery about it, man. It's full of thorns and sass, and I'm willingly throwing myself to the devil for a glimpse of happiness. So, how do you think your Ari will fair with Lexi?"

"My Ari?" It comes out on a breath. "Ah, I don't know. Lexi can be pretty prickly, but she's been softer here in Vermont. Maybe the mountain air calms her. Do you think I should be worried for Ari?"

Shit. I didn't really think about this.

"Nah, Lexi always befriends the fractured ones. She has it in her to be nice, she just guards that part of herself."

"She's more broken than we thought, huh?"

The sigh that Easton exhales is enough to bring me to my

knees. The pain in his eyes as he speaks shows the depth of what's happening between them.

"You know how Ash will recover from his physical wounds, but it's his emotional ones we're all worried about?"

"Yeah," I reply cautiously. Ashton's wounds, both emotional and of the flesh, are a guilt that weighs heavily on my heart.

"Well, imagine carrying those around but not letting anyone in. Harboring that pain all alone and believing it was your fault. Then multiply it by ten, and that's about where Locket is right now."

"Locket?" Curiosity finally wins, and I can't help but ask.

"Shit. Sorry, I … yeah. Locket. She's locked so far away, sometimes I don't know if I'll ever get through to her."

"Seems like you've made it further than most? From what I'm gathering, even Lanie's in the dark?"

"Yeah. That tends to happen when one little mistake in Vegas follows you home."

"Care to elaborate?" I smirk. There are only so many mistakes in Vegas that can follow you home.

"No, I don't. But for the record, *mistake* is Lexi's word, not mine."

This has my attention. "Whatever happened in Vegas has changed you both, that's for sure."

"I guess. So, should we head into town before Lexi runs your girl off?"

My girl? The more times he says it, the more it just sounds right. My soul is still at war, but I feel lighter than I have in years. That has to count for something, right?

CHAPTER 8

ARI

How the hell do I not have any water or electricity? *This cannot be happening right now.* Thank God Seth didn't come in. As I shine my cell phone light at the fuse box, I have a sinking feeling in my gut that my stepmother is responsible for this.

Bang. Bang. Bang.

I know without even looking that it's Virginia beating down my door. I haven't been home for half an hour, and she's ready to berate me. Shit. *Oh, Daddy. How long do I put up with this to keep you close?* Inhaling deeply through my nose, I let it out slowly before unlocking my front door. As soon as the bolt engages, the door flies open.

"Where have you been? How dare you leave our livelihood to go whoring around town? Not to mention, your sister was attracted to that man. Do you have no loyalty to those that keep a roof over your head?"

"Virginia, I—"

"How would your father feel knowing you paraded your slutty behavior all over town while you left his blood, sweat, and tears to some senile town gossip?"

"First of all," a voice cuts through Virginia's, causing us

both to turn; Virginia's face goes pale as Lexi Heart walks through the door with GG trailing behind, "GG isn't senile. Town gossip? Absolutely, but not senile, and she is two seconds away from announcing to the Town Cryer exactly how you treat your stepdaughter. Your stepdaughter, who, by the way, serves the locals every damn day while you lay on your ass doing nothing but collect a check."

"What in the crotchety cooch is this place?" GG asks in disgust. "Ariana Winters, tell me ya ain't living out here?"

Oh, God. I'm dreaming, right? This is not real. Covertly, I pinch myself, and damn, it hurts. This is happening. Suddenly, I'm thankful the sun is setting. No one can see my mortification, but I may lose the store altogether if the Heart women piss off Virginia. I'm not ready for that, not yet.

"It's ... It's—"

"It was her choice," Virginia states.

"Ari, why aren't you in your house?"

"Eck. It's my house, Rosa. Mine."

"Is that right? That's funny, because I seem to remember introducing Ari's mother to the McDowells right after she was born. Lilly was looking to have a will drawn up. Now, I don't know what all was in it, but you can bet your ass the McDowells will remember." GG's smile hides a witty, sharp mind you can see working overtime.

Daring a peek in Virginia's direction, I see she's gone ashen even in the dark. If she clenches her jaw any tighter, she might break a tooth.

"We covered that after Ian passed away," Virginia announces, but her voice wavers unnaturally.

Narrowing her eyes, GG takes a step forward. Never taking her gaze off Virginia, she speaks to me. "I think we'll need to take a visit to see Mimi McDowell first thing in the morning. But, Dissy, you haven't explained why you're livin' in this hut? John told me it was true, but I didn't believe him 'til right now."

"It's not that bad, GG," I sigh, embarrassed.

"Ari, there are no windows. Do you even have heat?" Lexi asks, spinning in a circle.

"I had a heater, yes. It's too hot for it now." I don't mention why we're standing in the dark.

"Yeah, because this is a glorified shed, not something you're supposed to live in," Lexi comments. "Do you even have power?"

"She's a grown woman," Virginia huffs, cutting Lexi off and conveniently avoiding the electricity question. "She can live wherever she chooses."

"That she can, Ginny, that she can. I'm thinkin' she'll be feeling right at home in no time at all," GG threatens.

"My girls need me." Virginia complains. "Ari? Make sure you're at work tomorrow. Do not make a habit of skipping out on your responsibilities, or it will force me to make drastic changes to our current situation."

This is a threat I'm used to. But I'm not used to someone sticking up on my behalf.

"I'd say go ahead and make those arrangements, Ginny, and don't let the door hit ya on your way out."

"What?" My voice is a few octaves too high, and Lexi lays a hand on my forearm in comfort.

"Trust us," she whispers.

"How dare you?" Virginia scoffs, but quickly retreats.

After she slams the door behind her, GG takes a seat on my bed because it's the only place to sit in my four hundred square feet. Lexi is quick to prop open the door to allow the last rays of daylight to illuminate the small space.

"Now, seems like we've got some things to work out," GG says, pulling her phone out of her pocket.

I watch on as she types far faster than I'd expect a woman of her age to do. *Can she even see what she's texting?*

"All right. First thing tomorrow morning, you have a meeting with Mimi McDowell. She will sort this all out for ya. Now, about livin' out here? Tell me the truth, was this your choice? If it was, I won't go pushing ya. Everyone's entitled to live how they want, but I've gotta feeling this was the wicked witch's doing. Am I right?"

Three years of pain crash into me, and my eyes prick with tears as I shake my head no.

"Just as I thought. Okay, let's get ya packed up," GG announces, but Lexi is already in motion.

"Wait? What? Packed up to go where? I can't leave, GG. This is all I have left. It's my only connection to my parents. If I'm not here, who knows what Virginia will do."

"That catty cow won't do a damn thing. It may take some time, but I know Mimi will take care of this. Just you wait. In the meantime, you'll come home with us. The lodge is a mess 'cause the roof caved in, and Easton is fixin' it up, but it's a home. We'll find a spot for you."

"But ... but, why? Why would you do this?"

"Because it's the right thing to do," Lexi says as though that's the most obvious explanation in the world. "GG's right, we're down to only a few rooms while the restoration work is being done, but you can either stay with me or go in the bunk room with Seth."

As if she conjured him by saying his name, Seth appears in the doorway.

"Oh good. Right on time," GG says, standing. "Come on then, we've got to get Dissy packed up."

"You're leaving?" Seth asks.

Is that alarm I hear in his voice?

"Ah, I ..."

"She's coming home with us," Lexi announces.

Seth's head is on a swivel at the moment as Easton walks in behind him and starts packing my few measly possessions into a suitcase Lexi found.

"Now, Dissy. I know what you're thinkin, but we're not strangers, and this is no place for you to live. You can come home with us or go to John's, but now that he's got all those roosters, you'll never get a wink of sleep over there. Not to mention all the cats he's adopted recently. It's a goddamn zoo over there."

I swear GG's a mind reader and a master manipulator because she just took away my one out. I can't go to Uncle Baker's because I'm deathly allergic to those feline beasts he insists on taking in.

Glancing around, I know staying here will end in disaster with Virginia on the warpath, but I truly don't have many options.

"Can you guys give us a minute?" Lexi asks.

"That's my girl." GG pats Lexi's hand as she escorts Easton and Seth out the front door.

"This is overwhelming. I get that feeling. Trust me, I get it. But I promise you, we want to do this, and before you ask, yes, we would do it for anyone. It's the Burke Hollow way, right?" She attempts to make me smile, but I feel out of control. "Listen, Ari, Easton knows adopted families better than anyone. His family sneezes, and they take in a new member. Seth's part of that whole mess now, too, and they take watching out for their own to the next level. So come home with us, let us help. Everyone needs a friend sometimes."

"I'm failing at life, Lexi." My hand flies to my mouth. I can't believe I just said that out loud.

"Me too, chica. Me too. We can fail together, how's that?"

Standing in a quickly darkening room, Lexi hugs me.

"Don't ever tell Easton I said this, but welcome to the chaos."

"Ha. I heard you, Locket," East bellows as he walks back inside. "I know you need some girl time, but we're running out of daylight. Ari? If there is anything you need tonight, we'd better get it packed up now while we can see."

GG's faster than I am and answers for me. "Take it all,

Grumpy. If ya don't, there's no tellin' what Ginny will do to it. Pack up both trucks, and we'll sort through it tomorrow."

"Yes, ma'am." Easton salutes.

I don't miss that Seth is silent. And brooding.

"Seth? Is … I'm sorry. Is this okay? It's been kind of a weird day."

He's in front of me in a few strides, his voice soft. "Of course. You can't stay here, Ri. I'm just sorry I left you here. How long have you been living like this?"

"I know it seems bad, but when the power was on, it really wasn't. I don't need much, Seth."

"She'll either have to sleep in my bed with me or go in the bunk—"

"She can sleep in the bunk room with me," Seth interrupts before turning back to me. "That's if you don't mind. Sorry. I shouldn't speak for you."

"No, that's fine. I don't want to put Lexi out. I really can sleep anywhere."

"We see that, Dissy. But we've got an actual bed for you at the lodge." I wince when I see GG lift the blankets to reveal my air mattress. "Let's get you out of here."

CHAPTER 9

SETH

I'm helping Easton with some sheetrock when I see GG pull up with Ari. She's been giving Ari a ride to and from work for the last few days. I think she's also been hanging out at the store to make sure her stepmother doesn't mess with her. Whatever magic GG wields, no one messes with her.

"You know, the sheetrock actually works better if you screw it to the wall."

Turning my head toward Easton's voice, I realize I've been holding a large piece in midair as I watched Ari.

"What's up with her?"

"What do you mean?" I ask him.

"So many choices." East chuckles. "Do you know what happened with the McDowells?"

"Yeah," I sigh. "There was a will, but her stepmother is contesting it. Mimi said if it gets tied up in court, it could be years before there's a resolution."

Easton crosses his arms over his chest. "So, what are we going to do about it?"

"What? I don't know that there's anything we can do."

"There's always something we can do," he says seriously.

"I used to call Ryan at EnVision for these types of problems, but guess who owns that now?"

Shit.

"That's right, buddy. You're part owner. I'd say this is right up Ashton's alley, and it might be just what he needs to return to the real world. Some food for thought anyway."

"Yeah, thanks. There's a lot of that happening lately." Setting down the sheetrock, I look to my friend.

"Guess it's time you decide what you want out of life and make it happen, man. Really think about what Rebecca would want for you and Sadie."

"I never dreamt I'd be a widower at thirty-two. I'm not sure how to move on," I admit.

"Saying good-bye is a good start."

I tear my gaze away from Easton because I know he's right, but am I ready?

~

The front door slams, and I poke my head around the corner to see Ari come in. I can tell by her expression something's wrong.

Dropping the hammer I was using, I make a beeline straight for her.

"Hey, what's wrong?"

When she finally makes eye contact, the part of my soul that's been fighting to get free unleashes in a flash of emotion. The need to protect this girl overrides every other rational thought. The unshed tears in her eyes slice through my chest and mark me as hers.

"Virginia closed the store. She changed the locks. I can't even get into the building. She posted no trespassing signs all over the property, and she called the sheriff when I tried to open the door."

Standing at arm's length, I crave to hold her. Fuck all the

polite bullshit we've been dancing around the last few days. I want to hold this woman. I desperately want to kiss her again, but for now, I pull her into my chest.

Her gasp goes straight to my cock. I bite my tongue and count to ten to get it to stand down. The last thing Ari needs right now is to feel my dick pressing into her belly.

"I'm going to fix this, Ri. I promise, I'll fix it."

She pushes back a little to look at me. "Don't make promises you can't keep, Seth. I know you're going home in a couple of days. You have responsibilities, just as I have them here. Plus, this is not your fight."

I want it to be my fight, though. *I want to fight for her*. The thought nearly knocks me over. There's so much to consider, and she's right. I'm leaving. I have Sadie. I have a new company and so many unanswered questions about my future. But fucking hell, if I don't see Ari as part of that future …

"I'm going to change," Ari announces, peeling herself out of my arms, and I feel gutted. I never want to let her go. "I think I'm going to go for a hike."

This has my attention. I haven't done anything on this mountain since I arrived except hang sheetrock and visit with the residents of Burke Hollow.

"Do you want company?"

She seems surprised, and suddenly I'm worried she'll say no.

"Er, sure."

"Don't sound so enthusiastic," I tease.

"It's not that, it's just … Never mind."

Watching her get flustered piques my curiosity, and I take another step toward her. When she backs up, a smile breaks free, and I take another step closer.

"What were you going to say, Ri?" My voice is husky and gives away the dirty thoughts running through my mind.

Furrowing her brow, she studies me. "I was just caught

off guard, that's all. I thought you've been avoiding me since GG roped you into kissing me."

That's not what I expected her to say. I have been giving her some space because her life is a shitshow right now. Everything came crashing down around her, and it was kind of our fault. Well meaning or not, there's no way around the fact that we upended life as she knew it. But I can't have her thinking it's because of that kiss.

My timing fucking sucks. The more time I spend with Ari, the more I realize I should have dealt with my feelings about Rebecca a long time ago. Of course, hindsight is 20/20 and all that.

I take another step forward, so she's backed up against the wall. Hovering over her, I stare into her eyes, willing my words to come.

"I need to make some things clear. I wasn't avoiding you because of that kiss. That kiss has not left my mind since the second my lips touched yours. I've been giving you space because we basically bulldozed over your life. I just figured it was a lot to deal with all at once. I didn't want to overwhelm you."

"It needed to happen," she says softly.

Lifting her chin to face me, I take a second to memorize the unique aqua marbling of her bright blue eyes. She's breathtaking.

"I'm not avoiding you," I say honestly. "We both have a lot of shit to figure out, but I never make promises I can't keep. I'm going to get your house back, I promise you."

Her lips part, and my gaze is drawn to her tongue that darts out to wet them.

"I believe you, but I never wanted to be the damsel in distress."

"Sometimes, it's the damsel in distress who saves the hero without even knowing it."

She swallows, and I follow the movement of her neck.

What I wouldn't give to lick a line down it. Taste her. Feel her. Lowering my forehead to hers, I settle for breathing her in.

"You make me crave things I never thought I'd want again," I admit.

"Like what?" she whispers.

"Forever."

CHAPTER 10

ARI

We've been hiking for about twenty minutes in silence. After his confession of forever, Seth shut down. I haven't pushed him, but my mind is running wild. How can he be thinking about forever? We live a thousand miles apart.

When I get to the clearing, I'm so lost in thought I don't see the root of an old pine tree. I'm flying forward before realizing what's happening, and hit the ground hard with my ankle caught between the root and the earth.

"Ari?" Seth yells from a few feet behind me.

"Shit, that hurt," I groan and attempt to roll over.

"Stop, hold on. Don't move. Your foot is really stuck. Just give me a minute."

Seth drops the backpack he was carrying to untie my sneaker. Carefully, he feeds my foot through the root and begins administering some sort of first aid.

"Can you move your toes?"

I wiggle them but wince. It freaking hurts.

With careful pressure, he gently feels along the bones of my ankle that's already swelling.

"I don't think it's broken, but you've got one hell of a sprain."

"Awesome," I grumble. Glancing around, I realize we are at the top of the mountain, and I'm not going to be able to get down.

"Don't worry, let's ice it and then see how it is."

"Ice it?" I question, but he's already opening his backpack and pulling out a first aid kit. "Look at you. Who knew you were such a boy scout."

"No boy scout, Ri. SIA. We trained for everything."

I realize how much I don't know about this man, and it's crazy to me that I think I'm catching feelings for him.

"Oooh," I hiss as he applies the ice pack to my ankle.

"You okay?"

"Yeah, sorry. I'm not usually such a baby."

"You're not a baby. This is a nasty sprain. You're probably going to need crutches."

Great.

After he wraps an ace bandage around my ankle to secure the ice pack, Seth lays out a blanket and sets me down on it. He takes a seat next to me, and I know the moment he notices the view.

"Holy shit," he whispers as he scans the forest laid out below us.

Laughing, I tell him, "That's pretty much the same reaction I have every time I come here."

"It must be insane up here in the fall."

"This side of the mountain doesn't get many visitors. The ones who know about it are all locals, and we all tend to have our own favorite spots."

Leaning back, I rest on my elbows and take in the view.

"You know, this has always been my favorite spot in the whole world. It's so peaceful. My dad used to bring us up here all the time. My mom and I would paint while he just watched because he didn't have an artistic bone in his body, but he always praised our talent. Even when I was perfecting stick figures, he made me think it was the most beautiful thing he'd ever seen."

Seth lies on his side, propping his head up on one hand. "Do you still paint?"

I glance away before he can see the sadness that washes over me.

"Did I say something wrong?"

"What? No, sorry. It's just, painting is a sore subject sometimes."

"Because it makes you miss your parents?"

I pick at the sticks on the ground to avoid answering right away. Do I want to tell Seth that I can't afford anything, so paint supplies are a luxury I haven't had in a long time? He can't think any less of me than he already does, I guess. I mean, he found me living in a shed, for Christ's sake.

"What's going on in that gorgeous head of yours?"

I sputter, trying to form words. Did he just call me gorgeous? The urge to look behind me for some beautiful stranger is so strong that I do. But, of course, we're alone. It's the middle of the day on a Wednesday—everyone is at school or work.

Seth's laughter brings me back to the present. "Did you think I was talking to someone else?"

"Honestly? Yeah," I admit self consciously.

His forehead crinkles in the sexiest way as he stares at me. He lifts a hand to tuck my consistently wild hair behind my ear, and his palm lingers on my face. "Has no one told you how beautiful you are, Ri?"

"It's been a while," I confess.

His gaze is so intense it causes butterflies deep in my core, and I clench my thighs together. *God, why do I have such a reaction to this man?*

Slowly, Seth leans forward, and I get the impression he's fighting with himself again. Feeling as though he's about to pull away, I lean into his touch to savor the lingering moments before he removes his hand. That slight movement seems to make a decision for him, and he pounces.

"I want to kiss you, Ri."

"I want you to kiss me."

"Thank fuck," are the last words I hear before his lips land in a bruising kiss.

CHAPTER 11

SETH

As soon as I taste her, something in me snaps. I nip and suck at her bottom lip until she grants me access, and I'm lost. Our tongues mingle gently at first while I savor the sweet taste of her. But it isn't enough.

Kissing a line from her lips to her ear, I nip her neck at the pulse point. When she moans, I nearly combust. Lowering my mouth to her ear, I whisper, "Ri, you're gorgeous." I kiss across her jaw to her other ear. "So fucking sexy."

"Seth," she pants.

"I want to touch you, Ri."

"God, yes, please." The need in her words mimics my own desperation.

"Where can I touch you?"

The rosy blush that creeps across her cheeks only makes me want her more.

"Where-wherever you want. Please, Seth, I … just please touch me."

Reaching down for the hem of her shirt, I tug on it until she sits up, and I pull it over her head. The sports bra she's wearing presents her perfect tits to me, and I want to run my tongue in the valley between. So I do. She's salty and sweet and so fucking addicting.

"Your tits are perfection," I groan as I cup each one. A perfect handful. Ari arches her back into my touch, and it feels like I just won the Super Bowl.

She reaches behind herself and undoes the clasp, and her breasts spill out into my waiting palms. Rosy little nubs harden at my touch, so I roll one between my thumb and forefinger.

"Oh my God," Ari cries out. She's loud, and it shocks the hell out of me, but I love it.

"If I keep this up, will you cry out my name, Ri? Are your nipples so sensitive that you could come just like this?" Her back arches again, and I notice she's rubbing her thighs together, seeking the friction I want to give her.

Leaning in, I growl into her ear, "Is your clit throbbing for me, sweetheart?"

"Yes! Yes, Seth."

Ari's hands fly out, tearing at my shirt, so I lift it over my head and toss it to the ground. She goes for my belt buckle next, and I expect a wave of panic to hit, but it doesn't. I'm so fucking turned on, I'm not sure anything could stop me.

She climbs to her knees, and I see the pain flash across her face.

"You're going to have to lie still, sweetheart. You can't put any weight on your ankle."

"But I want to touch you."

Lowering my pants, I relish the gasp she emits as my cock springs free. Nothing makes a man harder than seeing the look of appreciation and hunger written all over his woman's face.

"I guess you're just going to have to let me do the work this time." I grin.

"This time? Pretty cocky, aren't you?"

Flexing my ass cheeks, we both watch as my dick bobs before her.

"Pretty sure I have a right to be." I wink but can't take another second of not touching her.

"I want to taste you, Seth."

Holy fuck.

"The feeling is mutual," I growl so fiercely it shocks even myself. "Are you okay with sixty-nine?"

"Yes. Stop talking and give me your cock." Her bluntness surprises me, and apparently herself, because the expression on her face is priceless.

Hovering so my lips ghost over hers, I lick each one. "I love that you're so vocal, sweetheart. I love that you need me as much as I you, but I have to be sure this is what you crave. Once I start, I'm not sure I'll be able to stop. Is this what you want, Ari? Do you want me?"

"So much, Seth. So fucking much."

I grin and kiss her twice more before positioning myself over her. She grabs hold of my shaft instantly, and I have to breathe through my nose to keep from coming right then. When I feel the tip of her tongue circling my crown, my hips flex of their own accord.

With my knees on either side of her head, I lower my mouth to her pussy. Licking up and down her seam over and over again, I finally push my tongue deep inside of her. She tastes so fucking sweet.

Spreading her wide open with my fingers, I flick my tongue over clit until I find a rhythm that has her breathing heavy on my dick.

"Hmm," she hums her approval, and the vibrations have my hips moving. Ari shocks the hell out of me when she takes me deep and hums again. It takes every ounce of willpower not to come down her throat. As it is, I have to pull back before I fuck her face hard.

"Sweetheart, stop. You have to ... fuck me."

She releases me with a pop, and I attack her clit with vigor. Sucking it into my mouth, I hold it steady with my teeth while my tongue flicks relentlessly.

"Seth, I'm going to come. Fuck, Seth. Seth. Seth."

Ari's legs shake uncontrollably as her orgasm hits. I don't relent until I've licked every ounce of pleasure out of her I can. As she comes down from her high, I reach for the first aid kit and quickly suit up. I've never been so thankful for a condom in my whole damn life.

Positioning myself at her entrance, I wait for Ari's eyes to come back into focus.

"Are you ready for me, sweetheart?"

"Yes. Fuck me, Seth."

I don't need to be told twice. I enter her in one thrust and know I'm not going to last long. Her walls spasm at the intrusion, and my dick throbs inside of her. Easing out slowly, I watch the point of connection. As I ram back in, I'm lost in sensations, but it's when I make eye contact with Ari that I truly lose myself.

My eyes never leave hers as I move in and out, and I know I won't be able to walk away from her. It makes zero sense, and I have no idea how to make it work, but I know I'm going to try.

Ari cups her tit and pinches a nipple as I pick up my pace. When her hand snakes down her body and lands on her clit, my spine tingles with the first sensations of release.

"God, it's so sexy watching you touch yourself."

Her hand moves faster, and her breathing becomes shallow.

"Are you ready to come again, Ri?"

Biting her lip, she nods her head. Adjusting my angle, I lift her ass off the ground for leverage and thrust up and in. I'm so much deeper like this, and she combusts around me. Her walls strangling my cock is the last straw, and I come as an animalistic sound of pleasure erupts from the back of my throat.

We're frozen, staring at each other as we work to regulate our breathing. I'm at a loss for words. Sex has never been like that for me. So many emotions fight for top billing as I ease out of her. Quickly, I tie off the condom and toss it to the ground. Laying back, I pull her into my side because words still escape me.

With her head resting on my shoulder, she runs her hand through my smattering of chest hair. "Are you okay?"

Pulling my head back, I turn her to face me. "Yeah, I'm okay. Are you? I mean, this was … I wasn't planning. It just …"

Nodding, she says, "I know." I can't tell if it's sadness or tiredness in her voice, and I feel like an asshole. Who the fuck takes a woman for the first time on the ground in the woods?

We lay in silence for so long I fall asleep. When I wake, Ari's dressed and sitting on a rock off to the side, staring out at the mountainside. With her knees tucked into her chest, she appears so young. This image of her once again reminds me of my douchebaggery.

I dress quickly and take a seat next to her.

"Sorry I fell asleep," I say sheepishly. "How did you get over here?"

She smiles, but it doesn't reach her eyes. There's sadness there, and I hate that I might be the cause of it.

"It's okay. I fell asleep, too. I hobbled over. My ankle is sore, but it isn't too bad."

Taking her hand in mine, I watch her face for a reaction but get none. "Ri? Are we okay? I'm sorry, I—"

"No apologies, and no commitments, Seth. I knew what I was getting into. You don't have to feel guilty. I wanted this just as much as you did."

Then why do you look so fucking sad? I want to scream but don't.

No apologies and no commitments? What the fuck is that? And why do I feel like that's exactly what I need from her?

"We should probably start back. It's getting late, and it'll take me twice as long to get down the mountain with this foot."

"You're not walking, Ri."

"What do you mean? How do you expect me to get down? We're not calling for help, my foot is not that bad."

"Then I'll carry you."

"Okay." She laughs. But I'm not joking.

After packing up the blanket, I shove everything into the backpack. Then I place it on her shoulders, squat down, and wait for her to hop on my back.

"Are you kidding me?"

"Either hop on, or I'll carry you down in a fireman's hold over my shoulder."

She's out of her mind if she thinks I'm letting her get down any other way. Finally, she hops on, and we slowly make our way back to the lodge.

CHAPTER 12

ARI

Showing up at GG's house on Seth's back caused quite the commotion. As soon as Lexi and GG heard I was hurt, they swarmed in like mother hens. It's been a long time since I've had anyone care for me, let alone dote on me. It was a little overwhelming.

After a big dinner and some laughs, thanks to Colton, everyone went their separate ways. I'm lying on the top bunk, staring at the ceiling in the dark, listening to Seth toss and turn below me.

Rolling over, I peek over the edge of my bed.

"Can't sleep?"

Seth sighs, and I feel the weight of his worries in that single breath.

"No, sorry. Am I keeping you up?"

"Nah, my brains working overtime, too."

"Want to talk about it?"

Now it's my turn to sigh. "I don't know, Seth. My life is pretty messed up right now. You asked me about painting earlier, and the truth is, I can't afford the supplies. Without school or the store, I'm literally homeless. See? Messed up.

What about you? Want to tell me what has you rolling around down there?"

"You," he states simply.

"I don't have any regrets, Seth. You shouldn't either. I know you're going home in a few days. I'm not your responsibility. I'm an adult, and I'll figure my shit out."

"Hey?" Seth's fingertips appear near my face, so I reach out and take his hand. "I don't have any regrets either. I just have a bunch of shit to figure out, too."

When he doesn't offer any other explanation, I take that to mean we're done talking. I attempt to pull my hand free, but he hangs on and gives mine a squeeze as he interlaces our fingers.

"My best friend, Loki, his fiancé writes romance novels."

"Ah, okay?" *Where's he going with this?*

"We all had to read one of her books after we lost a bet. She wrote about this couple who had a lot of obstacles to overcome, but they fell in love the first time they met. Their one true love. Do you believe in that?"

"Insta-love or that you have one true love?"

"Both, I guess."

"I think the heart has an endless capacity for love, but I think love is a choice. You can love a hundred people, but you choose to stay in love with someone."

I want to ask about Rebecca so much. It's on the tip of my tongue when he speaks.

"Rebecca didn't want anything to do with me at first. She hated the military. I had to really work to win her over," he says quietly.

Hearing about her is different from what I thought it would be, though. Hearing about Rebecca and knowing all she's missing out on makes me sad for them all.

"Was she your first love?"

"She was my first everything. Ari?"

"Yeah?"

"I was okay on my own … until I met you, I thought I was happy."

"Whoosh." I let out a long breath, unsure I want to ask this next question. Eventually, I do. "And now?"

"I think I want more, but I don't know how to make that happen for everyone."

I nod, even though he can't see me.

"Tell me about Ari Winters?" he pleads, obviously needing a break from his own thoughts.

So I do. We talk all night, hand in hand, about our lives, our dreams, our fears. And when I wake up in the morning, Seth is nowhere to be found.

Climbing down the ladder proves more difficult with my tender ankle, but I manage. After getting dressed, I hobble out to the kitchen, and realize how late it is. *When is the last time I slept in?* Then I notice the table and an enormous pile of paint supplies. Not the cheap, drugstore supplies either. These are professional-grade, and way nicer than anything I've ever owned before.

The note on top says, **Ari**. Glancing around, I try to listen for movement, but the lodge is silent. I notice even Easton's constant hammering, sawing, and banging has ceased. Running my finger under the seal, I open the envelope.

Dear Ari,

Paint your future. Not the one you think you deserve, but the one you dream of. Then we'll make it happen.

Seth

"What the hell?" I murmur.

"Seth?" I call out but get silence in return. I make my way through the lodge but find no one.

"There ya are. You ready to meet Mimi? Sounds like she's got some good news for ya," GG says as she enters the lodge.

"Um, yeah. Have you seen Seth, though?"

"Hmm. Ya know, I haven't. Come to think of it, his truck was gone when I went out to feed the chickens this morning.

Ah, looks as though he went shopping, huh? I can't wait to see you paint, Dissy. Your mother always said she could paint, but you were the true talent. Maybe ya can paint me somethin' after your meeting, huh?"

"Sure, of course. I'd be happy to," I lie. I'm nowhere near as talented as my mother, so the compliment always hits differently. Seth's note has left me with an unsettled feeling, too, and that's all I can focus on.

"What's botherin' ya, Dissy?"

"Ah, nothing. I'll just get dressed, and we can leave. Thank you so much for driving me."

I turn to go, but GG stops me with a hand on my shoulder. "We all need family, Ariana. People who have your back. People who love you unconditionally and support you always. We can be your family, hun. You just have to trust us sometimes. Mimi will sort out your house, and in the meantime, you'll stay here as long as you need. My only stipulation is you take some time to figure out who Ari is and who she's gonna be."

Her little speech has me blinking away tears.

"You're gonna be all right, Dissy. I promise, just trust us to help you, okay?"

Without a second thought, I launch myself at the older woman. "Thank you, GG."

"You got it. We'll put you to work for Summerfest, don't you worry. I've got a plan for ya. Now get your ass in gear. Mimi's waitin'."

I can't help but laugh. GG always seems to have a plan, and if Lexi's right, she's four for four in her *plans*.

~

"Does that all make sense to you?" Mimi asks. This poor woman has been going over details with me for almost two hours to make sure I understand everything I'm about to sign.

"I think so," I say hesitantly.

"As your lawyer, I believe this is your best option. You're so young. This will give you income to finish art school if that's what you want or do something else entirely. As your friend, I'm telling you, the Westbrooks are some of the best people we have ever met. Our Julia married into that family. Well, sort of. What do they call it, GG? Family adjacent? I don't know. Her husband has known the Westbrooks since he was in diapers, and I've gotten to know them all very well over the last few years. They're honest and fair and are really looking out for you here."

"I guess that's the part I don't understand. I've met Easton since he's been here, but they don't really know me. Why would they go to all this trouble?"

Mimi and GG exchange a look that doesn't go unnoticed.

"'Cause Seth asked them to, Ariana. They're all on your team. You're special to Seth, and that makes you special to them. Even if Seth doesn't realize the extent of it yet, he will. Mark my words."

"Seth asked them to lease out the ground floor of my building, manage the store there, and refurbish it?"

"Yup. He also asked them to turn the upstairs into a rec center for art classes if that's what you want."

"But who would teach art classes?"

Mimi smiles kindly, like you would at a small, confused child. "You, dear. You would teach the art classes."

"What?" I screech. "B-But he's never even seen me paint. I haven't finished school. Why would he do that?"

"Because he believes in you, Ari. We all do."

"Wh-What about Virginia and the girls?"

GG's cackle startles me, and I almost fall out of my chair. "Well, that's the best part now, isn't it? Turns out, your dad did leave her the store. Do you know what the store consists of?"

I'm almost scared to ask.

"Products. That's it. She's entitled to groceries." GG is laughing so hard now I'm afraid she'll have a heart attack.

"Easton is waiting for you down there. He thought you might want to tell Virginia why she needs to be out by the end of the day."

"And don't go feeling guilty about this either, Dissy. That piece of work had the balls to come to Mimi and try to get the will nullified. Then she went a forged a whole lotta legal papers. She deserves everything comin' to her."

"But Easton is putting out so much money. How does this benefit him?"

GG stares at me for a long moment. "The Westbrooks are billionaires, Ari. He will tell you himself, this is a drop in a bucket for him, but it benefits them because it's an investment in you. It's an investment in this town, and between you and me, I have a feelin' he's sticking around here for a while."

"All because Seth asked him to?" I say more to myself than anything.

"Yup. Mark my words, Dissy. Good things are coming this way."

I'd love to believe her, but it's my experience when something seems too good to be true, it usually is.

CHAPTER 13

ARI

GG pulls up in front of the building that will soon be mine. Or mine again, I guess, and I notice my hands are shaking.

"Ya know, you don't have to be the one to do this, Ari. Easton is on standby, ready to escort the wicked witches out."

"What if she won't leave?"

GG points behind her, so I turn to look. The sheriff is sitting in his car, apparently waiting for us.

"Seth musta been up all night getting this information, but Easton promises, once she hears the news, she'll be ready to skip town as soon as possible. She's been stealing not only from you but from the state and federal governments, too. The law doesn't look kindly on people cashing checks of dead people."

"He did all this last night? How did he find this out? Where would he even get this information?"

"That's what they do, Dissy. Seth's a superspy, and he used his powers for good. Now come on, let's go take out the trash."

That makes me laugh. "I don't understand. If Seth did all

this, why isn't he here?"

"Now that I don't know, but I'm sure he'll explain himself soon."

"Yeah, okay. Here goes nothing."

I walk up the front steps I've known my entire life. I see the corner where I cut my head open after tripping over something. I see the planters my mother picked out whose flowers haven't sprouted yet. I see my home. This is my home, and I'll be damned if I let Virginia stay one second longer.

Easton has walked up beside me, a bunch of papers in hand, as the sheriff knocks on the door.

"You can do this, Ari," Easton whispers as Brittany opens the door.

"Mr. Westbrook, I'll be waiting in the car. If you end up needing my assistance, just wave a hand," Sheriff Dean states while shaking Easton's hand.

"I appreciate that, sir. Ari, you're up."

"What the hell is going on here?" Brittany asks while snapping gum like an eighties teen.

"You're in my house, and it's time to get the fuck out," I say simply.

Easton chuckles beside me.

"What is the meaning of this?" Virginia asks, finally coming to the door.

"You're probably going to want to do this inside." I watch as Easton hands her a piece of paper. Her hands shake as she steps back into the entryway.

I only half listen as Easton lays out all her misdeeds and what it will mean for all three of them if they don't agree to his terms. My mind keeps circling back to Seth's note and why he isn't here.

"I can't get a lifetime of stuff out in just a few hours," Virginia screams.

"Lucky for you, I'm generous." Easton smirks. "We've

hired a moving crew for you. They'll pack everything up and drive it wherever the hell you want. I've even gone above and beyond and booked you a room tonight, so you have time to sort out your next steps."

"How very generous of you," she spits.

Brittany and Tiffany have been unusually quiet. It makes me wonder how much of this they even understand.

Virginia's sudden movement catches my attention a fraction of a second too late. Her open palm lands on my cheek with so much force it knocks me back a step. Easton is on her a second later, but I hold up my hand to stop him. Now that I know it's coming, I'm prepared. This is my battle.

"How could you do this to me, you ungrateful, little bitch?" she hisses.

As much as I want to lash out, I know it won't make me feel any better. Because as I stare at her here with the realization that she's about to lose everything, all I feel is sadness. Not sadness for her, but for what could have been.

"Our lives could have been so much different if you'd only tried to like me. Not even love me, but like me. When you came into this house, I was just a child—a child who had lost her mother and was just looking for someone to be on her side. You chose hatred and cruelty instead. Don't you know it's so much easier to choose love, Virginia?"

"What the hell do you know about love, you stupid girl? I loved your father, but he could never love me because the ghost of your mother resided here every day in the form of you. You think one of these rich men is going to love you? You think they'll take care of you? It's all a bunch of bullshit, Ariana. They all leave eventually or trade you in for a younger model, and then you'll be right where I am today."

"That's where you're wrong, Virginia," I spit the words with years' worth of bitterness as I take three steps forward. Standing only inches apart, my stepmother looks at me with fear instead of disgust. "I'll never be like you because I'll always choose love. If I'm ever lucky enough to be a mother or a stepmother, I'll choose love. Life is all about choices, Virginia, and you chose wrong."

As I say the words, Seth and a faceless little girl pop into my head. I know what I've just said is my truth. I will love any child that graces my path.

Turning to Easton, I let him know I'm done here and walk out the door, leaving them to pack up their lives and leave mine for good. I should feel excited or happy, ecstatic even, but all I have in my chest is a lingering sense of dread.

I climb into the cab of GG's truck, and she gives me a solid hug. "Things will get better, Dissy, trust me."

"Okay," I reply, only because I'm too tired for anything else.

When we get back to the lodge, I find Lexi in the kitchen.

"Hey, Lexi. Have you seen Seth?"

"Aren't you supposed to have crutches or something?" she asks.

"Eh, they're more trouble than they're worth. I'm doing better, anyway. I'll put it up when I get back to the store. I still can't believe Virginia is out."

Begrudgingly, she acknowledges, "Yeah, Easton can do good sometimes, I guess."

"I still so confused, though. I really need to talk to Seth. Have you seen him? I haven't been able to find him all day."

The open-mouthed, blank stare she gives me makes my stomach drop.

"Um, he didn't tell you?"

Lexi is always confident. Her unease is setting off alarm bells.

"Tell me what?"

"Fucking asshole," she mumbles. "Ari, I'm sorry. He went back to North Carolina this afternoon."

I blink slowly as my brain tries to compute what she just said.

"He what?"

She shakes her head, and then rubs her temples. "He went home, Ari. I'm sorry. I can't believe he left."

Why would he go to all this trouble just to leave?

Realizing Lexi is still staring at me, I pull myself together just enough to get out of here with what's left of my dignity intact.

"Yeah, me either. I guess that's how it works, though, right? You sleep with someone, and they ghost you?"

She winces at my confession.

"I don't think that's—"

I hold up my hand to stop her. I'm not interested in hearing her come up with excuses for him. My chest constricts painfully as it sinks in.

Maybe this is just what men do. Love 'em and leave 'em, right?

"And here I was thinking I was catching feelings. I should have known. Feelings don't happen because of one kiss or a few days together. Obviously." I force a laugh. "So, I guess the girl thing to do is block him now?"

I have to get out of here. The last thing I want to do is cry in front of Lexi.

"Ah, you know what? I've gotta go. Thanks for everything, Lex. I'll call GG later and thank her, too."

"Ari, don't—"

"I need to go, please." My voice is shaky, and I can't hold back the tears. "Just ... I was stupid, Lexi. So freaking stupid to think—I don't know what I was thinking, actually. I just need to go home."

"For what it's worth, I know he has feelings for you. And, I do think when you meet the right person, love can happen instantly."

"Haha. Well, I'll let you know if I ever meet that person. I guess GG was wrong about this one. I gotta go. Thanks, Lex."

I cannot get off this mountain fast enough. As soon as I get outside, the tears flow freely.

CHAPTER 14

SETH

Lexi: Please tell me you're not that big of an asshole?

Preston: Ah, there's a lot of us on this thread. You're going to have to be more specific.

Lexi: Seth. Seth cannot possibly be this stupid.

Colton: *Running to get popcorn*

Easton: ...

Lexi: Don't say it, East.

Lexi: I'm serious. If Seth is this big of a jackass, I'll kill him.

This doesn't sound good.

Seth: I've been gone for six hours. What could have happened in six hours?

Lexi: THAT is what you did, you dingle dick!

Seth: What?

Lexi: For Christ's sake, Seth. You don't sleep with a girl and then leave the STATE without saying good-bye unless you're planning to never see her again. WTF???

Colton: Who did he sleep with?

Loki: Wait, what? Dude, seriously?

Halton: Even I know that's a dick move.

Easton: GG gave him a name.

Preston: SETH! You got matched, slept with her, then left without a word?

Seth: Can we not do this over text with everyone chiming in?

My phone rings before I can get out another text.

"You fucking asshat. What were you thinking?" Lexi yells.

"Lexi, I don't understand what you're so pissed off about. I have some shit I need to take care of so I can see if there's a future with Ari."

"You didn't think to maybe, I dunno, *tell her that*? She thinks you're gone, done, forever."

"What? Why would she think that? I left her a note."

"Oh, my God. You're an idiot. You slept with her, then skipped town. Your note didn't say anything about leaving or coming back."

Lexi is as angry as I've ever heard her. How did I fuck this up so epically?

"Okay, I'll call her."

"It's too late for that, dipshit. Ari thinks you ghosted her. She blocked you and won't take anyone's calls right now."

"She blocked me? That's ... fuck. You have to talk to her for me then, Lexi. I'll get back there as soon as I can."

"I've tried. Seth, you have to remember, she's lost nearly everyone in her life that loved her. She, well, she said she thought she was catching feelings. If you don't feel the same way, leave her alone. Let her figure her life out without stringing her along."

"I wouldn't do that, Lexi. I'm not fucking Miles." As soon as I say it, I regret it. "Lexi, I'm sorry—"

"Yeah, it's fine. Just figure your shit out, Seth, okay? Don't come back here just to break her heart all over again unless you want me ripping off your balls and feeding them to the chickens."

"Lexi—" the line goes dead. She hung up on me. Not that I blame her.

Fuck me. I only came home to make things right, so I could move forward. I plan on going back. I even told Easton I'd be back in a few days. My phone buzzes in my hand, and I see a text message from Loki.

Loki: Sounds like you're going to need the help of Prince Charming.

One of Loki's childhood friends, Dexter Cross, is the real-life Prince Charming, or at least he acts like he is with all his over-the-top, grand gestures that help a guy get the girl.

Seth: I'm all set, but thanks.
Loki: I'm happy for you, man.

I know what he means. He's been telling me for a while that Rebecca would want me to be happy. Maybe I'm finally ready to listen.

~

The drive to the cemetery doesn't take long, but I remain conflicted. I bounce between saying goodbye to Rebecca so I can move on, then worrying that I may have already ruined things with Ari before they even really began.

Entering the long, narrow road that leads to where Rebecca rests, I'm strangely calm. It's been too long since I've been here. I need to make more of an effort to bring Sadie, even if it's hard answering her never-ending questions.

I pull off to the side of the road, park behind another car, and climb out. The quiet here always unnerved me, but today I feel different. Making my way through the headstones, I stop short when I see a man standing at Rebecca's.

Loki.

I'm not surprised. They became good friends over the

years, but I know he's here for me. I inch forward until I hear his voice.

"Remember the family I told you about? The one that adopted me after my parents died? Well, they've taken in quite a few of us over the years, and now Seth and Sadie are part of the chaos. Sadie has a basketball team worth of *cousins,* and everyone adores her. Seth is also adjusting pretty well, but I'll let him tell you about that. My point is, they're in good hands, Becs. They are loved and happy, and we'll always take care of them."

I'm beginning to feel as if I'm intruding, so I turn to give him a few minutes alone.

"Don't leave on my account," Loki announces over his shoulder.

Of course he knew I was here. We had the same special ops training. He probably knew I was here before I got out of the car. He always was the better op.

"Have you been here long?"

Loki turns to show his shit-eating grin.

"Well, when I learned how miserably you fucked up GG's match, I knew you'd be here soon. I got here just before you. I thought you might need some backup, and it's been a while since I talked to Becs."

This man has had my back since basic training. I literally owe him my life ten times over.

"Sit with me?" I don't trust myself to say more right now. Emotion is a tough bitch who's grabbing at my throat.

Loki's smile only grows as he reaches behind him and pulls out two beers and a tiny bottle of rosé, Rebecca's favorite.

"I was hoping," he says, flicking the cap off the beers, then plopping down next to Rebecca's tombstone.

Seeing her name engraved in stone hits me just as hard as the day she died, and I freeze in a half crouch.

Rebecca Ann Foster

Loving Mother, Wife & Friend

I look away before I reach the date. A life cut far too short; the date is like a kick to the teeth.

We sit in silence while we drink our beers. Eventually, Loki unscrews the rosé and pours it into the ground.

"Salute," we say at the same time. None of us are Italian, but Rebecca insisted on saying it every time we got together.

"She'd be okay with this, you know?"

I nod, still too choked up to speak. Being here this time feels final. It feels real, and it hurts.

"Tell us about her." Loki nods toward the headstone, and a tear escapes. He doesn't give me shit, just pulls out a pack of tissues from his other pocket.

For some reason, that makes me laugh. "How much stuff do you have in those pockets?"

He joins in the laughter, then claps me on the shoulder. "We're family, Seth. I knew today would come, and I also knew it would be hard. Maybe even harder than the day we buried her, and I'll never let you go through something like this alone. The Westbrook mantra isn't just words. It's our way of life whether your last name is Westbrook, or Kane, or Foster. We take care of our own."

Opening the tissues, I catch movement in my peripheral vision, and my mouth drops open. Preston Westbrook is walking toward us with his friend, Dexter, at his side. That's when I notice Ashton trailing behind them. I can't fucking believe it. He's using a cane but walking of his own accord, and he's out in public, something I know Sylvie hasn't been able to convince him to do yet.

I glance at Loki for an explanation as this big, messy family made up of friends surrounds us. He just shrugs and waits for Ashton to join the circle. I'm so shook I can't even stand up, so everyone takes a seat next to me.

It takes Ash a while to get to the ground, but when Preston tries to help him, he nearly takes out his kneecaps with his cane. Once he's situated next to me, I notice his facial scars are not as prominent, but they are still very visible, and I lose my shit. One package of tissues isn't going to cut it.

Through my sniffling, I hear a garbled noise, and it takes me a minute to realize it's Ashton speaking. His voice is stronger than it's been, but the deep rasp he now carries will never go away.

As we all strain to hear him, Ash swallows, then tries again. "I thought it might help to show Becs that we have your back. You're not alone, Seth. We welcomed you to the chaos, and we will stand by you until our final breath." He shakes his head and points to Preston, the effort of speaking three sentences visibly taking its toll on him.

"Whether we're able to salvage your chance with GG's match ... Ari, right? Or not, we'll be here for it all. The good, the bad, and the ugly. You and Sadie are loved, forever. But, if I'm being honest, I'm inclined to think we can fix this because GG is scary as fuck about these things."

My eyes automatically dart to Rebecca's name as guilt fills my chest, but I nod yes. Leave it to Preston to ease the painful moment.

Preston rises and moves to stand in front of me. Not sure what to expect, I stand as well, and he wraps his enormous arms around me in a bear hug. I've heard about the Westbrook squeeze, but this is my first, and as corny as it sounds, it truly calms the ache in my chest.

"Okay, we're going to let you have some time alone with Rebecca now," he announces.

"What? You drove over an hour to sit here for all of five minutes?" I ask, staring at all of them.

"That's what we do, Seth. We travel in packs," Preston teases.

"He's not wrong," Dex interjects. "But seriously, we are giving you time to do what you came to do so you can hurry up and fix your colossal screwup in Vermont. The sooner the better."

"When the resident Prince Charming says you've fucked up, you better listen," Loki jokes. "We'll be at Sylvie's when you're done."

One by one, they all place a flower I hadn't noticed them holding on Rebecca's tombstone, then hug me in turn. Ash is the lone wolf that hangs back. I wonder if the guilt I feel over his condition will ever ease? Loki and I were trained for hostage situations. Ash should never have been that close.

When he leans in for a hug, he speaks again.

"We'll talk at my mother's." He turns to go, and I'm left alone with my thoughts.

A million different things run through my head, but I'm at peace. For once, I'm at peace.

"I hope you've found peace, too, Rebecca."

I spend the next couple of hours finally grieving the wife I lost, telling her how amazing our daughter is and about the future I hope to have. By the time I leave, I have resolution—Loki's right. Rebecca would want this for me. Now I have to figure out if I even stand a chance.

CHAPTER 15

ARI

I've spent the entire day in my pajamas eating Ben & Jerry's. Shockingly, I'm okay with that. I don't have anywhere to go or anything to do, so I've sulked. I really shouldn't be this sad. That's what I keep telling myself, anyway. I only spent a few days with the guy. *You slept with him. Then he skipped town.* Yeah, I can't forget that tidbit of information either.

"Ari? I hope you're dressed because I'm coming up." Lexi's voice startles me, and I drop my spoon.

Glancing down at myself, I'm almost embarrassed. I probably should have at least put on a bra.

"Well, you're mostly dressed," she snorts, walking into the living room. "Good thing no one locks their doors around here. It makes it that much harder to ignore me."

After setting the ice cream on the coffee table, I pull my knees up to my chest. It's probably best to just let her say her peace so she'll leave. I know she's on Seth's side. They run in the same circles. I'm just the small-town hookup.

"What's up, Lexi? If you came here to make an excuse for him, I'm really not in the mood to hear it."

"If you think I came here to do his groveling, you don't know me very well."

This surprises the hell out of me.

"If you're not here for him, why are you here?"

"Ari, you're my friend, too. Your entire world was just turned upside down. Why on earth would I let you go through that alone?"

"I just assumed you were on his side," I admit.

"There are no sides in this, Ari. I know you don't want to talk to him, and that's fine. I'm not here to push you. But Easton told me you're not sold on the rec center idea? How come?"

"I'm twenty-four years old, Lexi. I haven't finished school. I've never held a real job, and until Easton's rent checks start coming in, I have thirty-two dollars to my name. Why on earth would he ever think it's a good idea for me to run a rec center?"

She stares at me and smiles. "Because you're family, Ari. Family by choice, and I'm beginning to learn that can be even better than the real thing sometimes. You're talented. Everyone in this town knows it, except for you. Before your dad passed away, you were on your way to becoming the artist you were born to be. The wicked witch may have stolen that away for a couple of years, but don't let her take it away permanently. If you're holding back because of Seth, don't do that either. An opportunity is an opportunity, no matter how you got it."

Tears sting my eyes, but I can't look away from her.

"I think we're a lot alike in some ways, Ari. We've spent so much time alone, we don't know how to let anyone in. I'm trying to do better, and you should, too. I know he messed up, but Seth looked out for you because he cared for you. Use that knowledge to determine where you go from here, not the rest of it."

"I don't know the first thing about opening a rec center, Lexi. What if I screw it up?"

"Then the whole damn town will help you fix it. We all want to see you succeed, Ari. You have people in your corner cheering you on, but you must be the one who wants it. You're the only can that can take that first step."

I nod, and she comes in for a hug.

"You have a voice, Ari, and you have a choice. Choose happiness, however that may look to you. Life is too short to be anything but happy."

Lexi pulls back and seems shocked by her own words, but they ring in my head like an echo.

"And, Ari?"

I glance up when she doesn't continue.

"I know it isn't your nature to yell, or fight. You're a gentle soul, and that's why everyone loves you, but when you do see Seth again? Set your inner bitch free, he deserves it, and if you can't find her, just channel me."

"I get the feeling you're not really a bitch, Lexi."

"We are who we want to be, my friend. Sometimes self preservation outweighs all else."

I desperately want to know what haunts her, but she turns to leave before I can ask any questions.

I sit on the couch long after Lexi has gone home, but her words never leave my head. Out of the corner of my eye, I notice the bag with art supplies Seth left for me. With a heavy sigh, I get up and dump out its contents. Staring at the rainbow of colors, an idea comes to me.

After scooping up all the supplies, I run to my old room that is now bare. If I close my eyes, I can still see the murals my mother painted. I can still feel the excitement of holding a paintbrush. I remember what it felt like to have goals and dreams.

Without thinking, I squeeze paint into empty tins.

Picking up a paintbrush, I hold it to the wall. After a second, muscle memory takes over, and I start to create.

I don't know how long I paint for, but by the time I'm done, a new mural mixed with memories of the old covers every wall of the room. Staring at what I've done, I start to believe that this is what I'm meant to do. I try not to pay attention to the fact that the man in the mural looks suspiciously like Seth.

～

"The first floor will still be a country store, but we'll renovate and update the entire space. Up here, we can do whatever you want. Seth had mentioned turning it into some sort of rec center for the arts. Is that something you would want to do?"

"I wouldn't know the first thing about taking on something like that," I admit.

"Ari, by the time we're done with the lodge and all the other plans we have coming, you'll have an entire team at your disposal. Lexi said a rec center is something that's desperately needed around here, but I'll leave it up to you."

Thinking back on that conversation hurts a little. How could Seth be so thoughtful, then walk away?

My phone chimes, and I know it'll be Lexi again. Taking a peek, I see I'm right.

Lexi: Renovations start today! And Easton will be there in an hour so you can tell him you're ready to take on the rec center.

Ari: I haven't made up my mind yet, Lex.

Lexi: You will. You're stronger than you give yourself credit for. Just remember, we're all in your corner. You can do this. Luvs.

Her confidence in me causes me to smile. It's been a long time since someone believed in me. I've given myself a few days to be sad, but I need to get my shit together. I know Lexi was right. As close as Seth is to the Westbrooks, I know I'll see him again someday, and I will not be *that* girl sitting idly by, waiting for him.

Scrutinizing the man in the mural who is decidedly not Seth, I make my decision. In my heart of hearts, I know I can do this. And Lexi's right. With all the budget cuts to local schools, our community desperately needs a place for the arts.

I can be the one to give it to them.

I hear a loud thud, followed by Uncle Baker's voice.

"Ari? Where are you, girl?" he hollers from the bottom step.

"In the bedroom," I yell back.

"Well, get down here. I need help." Something else lands with a thud, and I fly down the hallway, worried he fell.

When I get to the stairs, I see he's bringing in large boxes from outside.

"What is this?"

"Presents. Carry them upstairs. I can only haul them so far."

"Presents for who?" I shriek. I certainly haven't purchased anything.

"For you, now get moving." God, he can be a bossy queen when he wants to be.

It takes four trips, but I finally get them all to the kitchen table.

"Sit," he orders.

Geez. He's in rare form today.

"Seth—"

At the mention of his name, I jump up, knocking my chair over in the process.

"Sit, sweetpea. I'm always on your team, remember?"

"I don't need a lecture about Seth, Uncle Baker." Crossing

my arms over my chest, I stare at the floor like an angry teenager.

"Good thing I'm not here to give you one, then. But, I am here bearing gifts, from him."

I don't miss that he doesn't say Seth's name this time.

"Now, there are three types of men in this world. The happy wife, happy life man. The destined to be single forever man, and the stupid man. Any guesses which type Seth is?"

"Er, I'm not really up for guessing games."

"Fine, I'll tell you. Stupid man. That's where Seth falls. Now, he wanted to tell you this himself, but it seems you're trigger-happy with the block button. Seth was always coming back, Ari. For you. He ran home to North Carolina because he had to sort through his own messy demons before he could fully move forward."

Rebecca comes to mind, and I feel a sense of guilt for falling in love with her husband. Record scratch, back that up. What did my subconscious just say? I was not falling. Was I?

Uncle Baker snaps his fingers in front of my face a few times, and I realize I zoned out.

"Sorry, what did you say?"

"He planned to come right back, but his daughter fell off the swing and broke her collarbone. He has to let her heal a little more before they can make the trip. But he is coming back with his daughter, and he's planning to stay indefinitely."

"What? How? Is she okay?"

"Yes, she'll be fine. And, I don't know the details, but I guess another Westbrook has some work to do here, and they're setting up shop in Burke Hollow. Now, I know I said I wasn't going to lecture you, but—"

I laugh. "There's always a but with you."

Uncle Baker sighs, and his serious expression scares me. I've only ever seen him like this twice before.

"I need you to really listen," he says earnestly. "Seth has a little girl who has lost her mom. You're still so young, but if you're going to see where things go with Seth, he's a package deal. You have to be sure you're ready to take on that responsibility because it won't be fair for her to fall in love with you only to lose someone else."

That is the last thing I was expecting, so I take a minute to respond.

"I-I hadn't thought about that, but you're right. Of course, you're right." *She's just like me.* "I can't help but think about how similar her situation is to my own."

He smiles sadly. "No one knows her pain better than you, but it's something to think about. Now, open these boxes. I'm dying to see what's in them."

Leave it to nosy Uncle Baker, but I have to admit, I'm curious, too. Grabbing the scissors from the counter, I slice open the first box, then the other three, and open the lids carefully.

"Oh, there's a note on this one." He grabs it and waves it in my face.

Do I really want to open this in front of him?

"Hurry up, Ari. I'm dying here." Fanning himself, I can tell he's trying to sneak a peek into a box.

"Fine. But I can't promise you'll get to read it."

Carefully opening the envelope, I pull out a single piece of cardstock.

Ri,

I fucked up. I was always coming back. I just had to make sure I could be the man you deserve first. It's taking longer than I expected, but I hope you'll give me a chance to grovel in person. In the meantime, paint your future, and hopefully, we can get there. Together.

Love,
Seth

"Love, Seth? He said love, Ari!"

Clutching the note to my chest in exasperation, I scoff. "I can't believe you read it over my shoulder."

"Oh, Ari, you've known me your whole life. What else do you expect? So, what did he send?"

Slapping his hand away as he opens the flap on a box, I lift out canvases in all different sizes. The last box contains an easel. He truly thought of everything.

"Paint your future, and we'll get there together," I whisper.

"Well, my job here is done. Looks like you've got some thinking and some painting to do."

I stand in my kitchen, speechless, as Uncle Baker kisses me on the top of my head, then walks out the door.

Staring at the note, I read it again. He did say love. Sinking into my chair, I run my fingers along the bristles of the brushes, then waste no time setting everything up. My entire body vibrates with excitement as I consider what to paint.

Paint my future.

Grabbing my phone, I turn on Apple music and get lost in my art. Three days later, I see my future clearly, and they're filling my kitchen.

CHAPTER 16

SETH

*A*fter the doctor places Sadie in a sling, we're released from the hospital. Surprisingly, I'm not as much of a mess as I thought I'd be. It happened so quickly. One minute I was pushing her on the swing set Sylvie just had installed, and the next, Sadie was going airborne. Even though I'm itching to get back to Vermont, I know we need to wait at least a week. Plus, Sylvie is a mess and insisted we come straight to her house so she can see Sadie herself.

Helping Sadie out of the car, I carry her gingerly to the front door, which opens before I can knock.

"Oh, my poor Sadie, look at you," Sylvie says with tears in her eyes.

"I's okay, Nanna Sylvie. It just hurts a little bit. But now Uncle Ash and I match."

"You're a sweet, sweet girl, Sadie Jane." Turning to me, she kisses my cheek. "Ash is refusing to stay in the hospital bed a minute longer. Why don't you go lay her down there?"

"Okay. Thanks, Sylvie. But you do know we have to go home sometime, though, right?"

"Eventually," she says aloofly.

I have a feeling she would lock us all up here living under

one roof if she could get away with it. I'm starting to understand why all my friends have turned out to be such amazing men. Everyone needs a Sylvie Westbrook in their corner.

The second I set Sadie down, the pain medicine kicks in, and she falls asleep.

"Ash is in the office with Loki. He wanted to talk to you when you got here," Sylvie informs me.

I'm surprised that he's up and moving around as much as he is. Hopefully, that's a good sign for his recovery.

"I'm off to talk to someone about childproofing the swing set."

I'm not sure I heard her correctly, but before I can question her, she's turned and left me standing alone in the hallway. Heading the opposite direction, I knock on the door to her home office.

"Come in," Loki bellows.

Entering the room, I find them sitting together over a bunch of papers, and Ash wastes no time jumping in.

"I know you're worried about EnVision, and your part in it, but don't. Loki and I have been talking. Something's not right. The Westbrook Group leaks. Pacen? Macomb? Dillon? They're all connected somehow, I just can't figure it out from here. I think we need to run this mission from Burke Hollow."

That bit of information has all my military training kicking in, and my heart fluttering like a schoolgirl. Then I notice Loki's forehead is creased. It's his only tell that something's wrong. Ashton nods, and Loki glances around, searching for unknown threats. I know that look well.

"Pacen Macomb has gone missing," Loki whispers.

I recognize the last name from my conversations with Easton, but Pacen doesn't ring any bells.

"We need to find her," Loki continues. "The last place she was seen was in Burke Hollow with her father and another man."

None of this makes sense, but I trust these two with my life. "Okay, fill me in."

Ash shakes his head, and Loki speaks for him.

"This won't be a quick open and shut case. I think Ash is right. The two of you need to be based in Burke Hollow, at least for a few months to figure out what the fuck is going on. I'll check in remotely and travel back and forth."

"Does this have anything to do with GG's mountain? Or the man Easton hates? Dillon Henry?"

Ash cringes at the name, but recovers quickly.

"We don't know why they're in Vermont yet, but I don't believe Dillon is involved the way you're thinking. We just need to find that girl."

I understand the need to find a missing person, but Ashton looks as though he could explode every time she's mentioned.

Acknowledging it can only mean one thing, I ask, "Why is she so important? What does she have that we need?"

"We're not sure yet," Loki admits, but we're both watching Ash. He has information he isn't sharing.

"Anything else we should be aware of, Ashton?"

"Not yet," he rasps. "I'll get you everything you need to know soon, though."

Loki and I exchange a worried look. Ash is barely able to move, but he's adamant about going to Vermont.

"Ash? I can handle it. You don't have to push yourself like this," I tell him.

He shakes his head wildly. "No. I will be the one to find her."

Knowing I have only one choice here, I put my faith in Ashton. We spend the next week pulling every detail we can find on Pacen Macomb.

CHAPTER 17

ARI

A noise on the stairs makes me stop. Easton's crew has been downstairs every day, but that's not—

A knock on my door interrupts my thoughts, and I open it, expecting to see one of the crew. Instead, standing before me is Seth, carrying the most beautiful little girl I've ever seen.

"Hi." He smiles. "You got your gifts."

Glancing down, I realize I've barely done anything other than paint for three straight days. Opening the door a little wider, I step to the side and usher them in.

"I-I did," I say as he passes.

"My daddy gives the bestest presents, doesn't he, Ri?"

I'm caught off guard that she knows my name, but I try to recover quickly. "I, ah, yes. Yes, he does."

"Did he give you the paints? I love, love, love to paint, but I broke my dog bone," she says sadly.

"You mean your collarbone, Sadie. You broke your collarbone."

She giggles, and I swear she just beamed sunshine my way like a cartoon bear.

"Honey, this is my friend, Ari. Ari, this is Sadie." He looks uneasy before continuing, and just as he had the day I met him, he starts to babble. "Ah, I know we haven't really talked about—"

His words stop short as something catches his eye. I don't have to turn my head to know what it is. We're surrounded by them.

He carefully sets Sadie down on a chair, then walks from painting to painting.

"Oh, Miss Ri, did you paint all these? They is better than the ones at the store." Her little brow furrows, so much like Seth's, as she stares at a painting across the room. "Hey, that one looks like Daddy." She points a chubby little finger, and we all turn.

When I started painting his portrait, I had a hard time finding my groove, and they came out abstractly because of it. As I got more comfortable, the images came into focus. The one Sadie just pointed to is the one I was working on just before they arrived.

"Is … is that me?" Seth asks, glancing around the room at the paintings of the same scene in various settings.

"Yes." My voice is shaky with nerves. "You said to paint my future."

Seth spins again, spending more time at each one.

After an excruciatingly long time, he turns a teary gaze to mine. "Tell me."

When I don't immediately answer, he asks again. "Tell me how you see your future."

"Hey!" Sadie squeals. "Daddy, Daddy, look. That one looks just like me." She glances from Seth back to the painting. "It looks like both of us, Daddy. You and me and …" She scrunches up her little nose, and I have the urge to wrap her up in a giant hug. "Miss Ri, is this you holdin' my hand?"

"How did you know what she looks like?" he asks quietly.

"I didn't. This is just how I pictured her."

"It is me, isn't it? Isn't it, Miss Ri? Did you paint me 'cause I was comin' to visit?"

Glancing at Seth for guidance, I watch as he makes a sweeping motion with his hands. I assume that means I can tell her.

"Honestly, I wasn't sure you were coming, sweetpea, but I was hoping."

"You is so good. Wait 'til Nanna Sylvie sees this. Can I call her, Daddy? Can I call Nanna Sylvie?"

"Knock, knock," Lexi says from the open door. "I thought I heard Sadie Jane was up here! Where is she?"

Lexi looks all around the room, but never drops her gaze to the little girl.

"Auntie Lex. I is right here. Right in front of you."

Lexi glances down, and I think I see a flash of pain cross her face. But as quickly as it appeared, it's gone.

"Oh, my goodness. I didn't see you down there. How's my favorite Sadie Jane?"

"I broke my dog bone," she says sadly.

Seth begins to correct her, but Lexi just smiles. "You know who is missing you the most?"

"Who?"

"GG. I heard you were here, and she sent me straight away to see if I could borrow you for a few hours. We need someone to supervise our cookie-making operation."

The little girl's eyes go wide as she pleads with her father without a word. How he ever says no to her is beyond me.

"Can I go, Daddy?"

"Sure, but remember the rule?"

"I has to stay very, very still so my dog bone can heal."

I can't help but laugh. You're probably supposed to correct things like that, but why would you when it's so stinking cute?

"Okay then. Listen to Lexi, and don't repeat anything GG says."

I stare at him with a raised eyebrow.

"Last time she visited, Sadie and Tate were running around saying they wanted a dingle dinky because GG told them it was a snack," he explains, and I burst out laughing. "Yeah, it's real funny until they go to school and ask for a dingle dinky."

"Oh my God." I clasp a hand over my mouth to control my laughter, but as Seth watches me, a grin I've never seen crosses his face.

"What?" I ask self consciously.

"If I could hear that sound for the rest of my life, I'd be a very happy man."

"And that's our cue to get out of here. We'll see you back at the lodge," Lexi says, helping Sadie off the chair.

Seth gives her a quick hug and a kiss, and then we're alone, with my paintings of the future I want surrounding us.

He must be thinking the same thing because he walks toward me on a mission. "Tell me," he demands. "Tell me what you painted."

Staring into his darkened eyes, I see my hopes and desires reflected back. "I painted a family."

"Just any family?"

Biting my lip as nerves suddenly take over, I shake my head. "No, not just any family, Seth."

"Who did you paint?"

Here goes nothing.

"Us. You. Me. And Sadie."

The broadest smile I've ever seen slowly sneaks across his handsome face. "You see us as your future?"

"I mean, there's a lot of stuff, like real adult stuff we need to figure out, but yes. When I picture my future, I see you. I see us, all of us."

He lunges, and his lips meet mine, but they aren't frantic.

They're slow, controlled. Measured. The longer he kisses me, the more deeply I feel him in my soul.

When he pulls back, we're still nose to nose, unwilling to separate completely.

"Do you think GG was right?" I ask against his lips.

"About us?"

"About us? About love at first sight? About soul mates?"

"I think she's a scary woman, and I don't ever want to be on her bad side. But, I think it's safe to say she's five for five."

Now it's my turn to grin like a fool.

"Seth, thank you for everything you did. I don't know how to express how much it means to me. I'm completely overwhelmed by everyone's generosity. This entire time, I've been racking my brain trying to figure out why you would do something so extraordinary for some you've only known a short time."

"Why I did it? Ri, I did it because you saved me."

I laugh at his ridiculousness.

"I'm serious." And by his expression, I can tell he is. "Ri, I think I started falling in love with you at our first dance. That first touch brought me back to life in a way I didn't think was possible. I'd been existing before you. After only three days, I knew I wanted to live again. I wanted to live because of you, for you, with you."

"You think you're falling in love with me?" I couldn't ask this question with a straight face if I tried.

His grin matches my own. "I know I am. Ashton and I are setting up a temporary office here, but it'll be months before we make any permanent decisions. So, you and I can take things one day at a time. But because I almost fucked this up once, I want to be very clear about something." I pull back when I notice the seriousness of his tone. "I am looking to make sure GG stays five for five in her quest for world domination by love match. Is that all right with you?"

I wrap my arms around his neck, and he lifts me clear off the ground.

"Yeah. I think that sounds like a very happily ever after."

"It will be, sweetheart. I promise you, it will be."

*See how Ari and Seth's love story develops in special cameos all throughout the Westbrook Series.

EPILOGUE

One Month Later

"My fucking back is killing me," Halt grumbles as he enters the kitchen.

I know the feeling. We're making progress in the other rooms, but none are inhabitable yet. GG's lodge is in worse shape than anyone imagined. With all of us here crammed into three bedrooms, they're taking turns in the bunk room.

I rented a small condo for Sadie and me. It helps that it is within walking distance of Ri.

"I don't understand why we can't just hire a freaking crew. This lodge would have been finished six months ago," Loki chimes in.

"GG's stubborn. She won't take our money, no matter how I approach her about it. Lexi isn't helping the situation either," East informs us.

"What are we going to do when the rest of the guys arrive tomorrow?" I ask East. "Three more grown men, their wives, and I lost track of the kids."

"They'll stay at the Wagon Wheel, but you're right, we need to do something. If you and Ash are going to be here full time, we need to start thinking about some Westbrook accommodations."

"Ho-Holy shit," Halton sputters. "That's it. I've got it!" He runs out of the room, only to return a few seconds later with a stack of papers. As he's laying them out on the table, we all crowd around to see what he has.

"GG's husband leased that land to Burke Hollow for seventy-five years, right?"

"Yeah, he wanted to keep it as open space for the town as long as he could," Easton confirms.

"But he put in a clause that if the town were to face financial hardships, they could develop a portion of it?"

We all stare at Halt like he's losing his mind. Maybe he is. Lack of sleep will do that to a man.

"We've already covered that, Halton." East doesn't hide his annoyance very well.

"Okay, but here's the thing. If EnVision is opening a security office here, that's bringing business to town. I'm willing to bet there will be a few Westbrook Group developments, too. Those will all bring jobs to the town, so they won't really be in a hardship anymore."

"I see where you're going, but that is a year or more out, Halton. Fontaine wants jobs now." Easton's tone goes cold at the mention of the old man.

"Anything Macomb brings will take at least that long. However, I have a solution. A way to keep the back side of the mountain an open space for the town without having to go into a bidding war with Macomb."

Easton looks over the papers, but appears as lost as I am.

"Benny Heart also put another clause into place." Halton's mischievous tone has us all turning toward him. "Nothing can be developed within an acre of a free-standing Heart building."

When none of us say anything, Halton grabs a map of the mountain and sets it on top of the papers.

"The Westbrooks are coming to town, right? Some of us," he pauses to look at Easton, "are probably here for good. With Dexter and Trevor coming back so often, wouldn't it make sense for us to have a few houses here?"

"Of course, but—"

"If we build houses crisscrossing the mountain, it will still leave most of the land as free space. It will also make it illegal for anyone to develop it." Halton leans back in his chair with arms crossed over his chest. "We need to get some crews to build us some houses."

"You think GG will go for it?" I ask.

"If it saves her mountain, I think she'll be all for it. And, we'll rent the land each house sits on from her. That will give her the money to fix this place up and we won't have to bust our asses to get it done," Easton adds.

"Is it legal though?" Loki asks.

"I'll ask Mimi to look at the contracts, but from what I can tell, it is still GG's property. The town only has rights to green space. It will take a town vote to determine it is in a financial hardship worthy of developing it. I'm almost positive she can do with it what she likes."

"We will have to move fast," East says seriously. "Summerfest is less than a month away."

"I'll talk to Mimi this morning."

Standing, Easton walks to the front door. "I'll go talk to GG. If this works, it'll be good for everyone."

As he reaches the door, it flies open, and Colton comes bouncing in. "Look who's home!" he yells animatedly.

He steps aside, and a petite brunette with bright green eyes enters.

"Holy fuck. Rylan?" Halt chokes out.

I turn just in time to see the chair he has perched on its back legs fall over, sending Halton crashing to the ground.

"Yup. She's finally home, and she agreed to come help out

for the summer. Isn't that amazing?" Colton's excitement is in complete contrast with Halton's behavior.

I glance between the two and notice Rylan hasn't taken her eyes off of Halt, but Colton is oblivious.

"Ry, this is Seth. You know everyone else."

"Ah, yeah. Of course. It's nice to see you all." Her voice is soft and uncertain as Easton approaches and wraps her in a hug.

"It's been so long, Ry. We've missed you. Freaking Colton has been lost without his best friend."

When he releases her, I hold out my hand. "Nice to meet you, Rylan."

"You too," she says quietly.

Loki gives her a hug as well. Then we all turn back, expecting Halton to offer a greeting, except he's nowhere to be found.

~

"How was your day?" Ri asks as I flip the burgers. She's been painting with Sadie and they're both covered in pink.

"It was good. Ash and I are hammering out details in between all the Summerfest shit Lexi has us working on."

"You know, it's really amazing you guys are all here helping like this. I've never seen anything like it."

Walking up to her, I wrap my arms around her waist. We have been very careful about how affectionate we are with each other in front of Sadie, but it's fucking hard.

"We take family very seriously, Ri." Glancing around, I see Sadie is occupied at her art easel, so I tug Ari behind a tree. "I need to kiss you," I growl.

"I missed you today," she admits, and I don't know what responds first—my heart or my dick. Both seem to run in overdrive every time she's around.

Just as I lean in to kiss her, I hear giggling behind me. Ari jumps back, but I don't let her get far.

"Kiss her, Daddy. Kiss her like the princes do," Sadie squeals.

Ari blushes crimson, but I know it's time to have the talk. Spending every day with Ari has only cemented my feelings. I'm meant to be with her.

"Would that be okay with you?"

"Oh, yes, Daddy. Daddies are supposed to kiss the Mommy." I hear Ari gasp, and I feel like shit. That is not what I was expecting Sadie to say, and it might be too soon for Ari to handle all this.

My eyes well with tears when she squats down next to my little girl, though.

"You know, sweetpea, some kids are lucky and end up with two moms, but it's important to know how much your mommy in heaven loves you."

"Are you gonna be my second mom?" Sadie asks innocently.

"It's too—"

"You know, right now I'm loving getting to know you. We have a lot to learn about each other, right? So, how about if we become best friends first, then down the road if you decide you'd like me to be your mom …" Ari glances up at me, and I smile. "Well, nothing would make me happier. But it has to be your choice, okay? What if I end up being like Cinderella's stepmother?"

Sadie giggles. "Oh, Miss Ri. You could never be like her. You already love me."

We watch as Sadie runs back to her easel and picks up a paintbrush.

"She's right." Ari chokes back a sob. "I-I do already love her. And you."

Holding out my hand to help her off the ground, I wipe

away an errant tear with my free hand. When I have her in my arms, I lean in for that kiss.

"I think I've loved you since our first dance, Ri. And today … well, today my world just became complete. I love you, sweetheart."

"Me too, me too," Sadie screams. "I loves ya both so, so much."

Glancing between my two girls, I know we're going to be all right. It seems the Westbrook adoptee program just gained another member.

Want to see where Seth & Ari are in three years? Download the extended epilogue, Three Years Later, Here!

If you loved this book please consider leaving a review.
Reviews are how Indie Authors like myself succeed.
Thank you!
Please leave a review here!

Avery hangs out in her reader group, the LUV Club, daily.
Join her on FB to get teasers, updates, giveaways and release dates first!
Avery Maxwell's LUV Club

**Turn the page for a sneak peek at
One Little Mistake, Easton's story.
Available Here!**

ONE LITTLE MISTAKE

PREVIEW

Easton
Eight months ago

"What?" I bark into the phone.

Caller ID tells me it's my older brother, Preston, but in truth, I would have answered the same way regardless of who it was. I'm a prick by choice. It keeps me safe, but I acknowledge I may have taken it too far with my last assistant. It's why I arranged a hefty severance for her, even though she quit.

"Hey, sunshine. Do you always answer your phone like a neanderthal, or is that a special greeting just for me?"

Preston is my oldest brother and has a circus happening around him right now. The fact that he's calling tells me he needs a favor.

"What do you need, Preston?" These are the times I miss having an assistant. Their job is to be my gatekeeper, even if it's my family. The only exception is my mother. No one fucks with Sylvie Westbrook.

"It's not what I need, asshole. It's what I have."

"I'm not in the mood for riddles. I'm swamped over here." My voice is flat with an edge of annoyance.

"That's what I'm calling for, East." Preston lets out a loud whoosh of air. "What happened to us, East? We used to be so close."

He's not wrong. Pres was my best friend growing up. Even though his three friends basically lived at our house, he never made me feel like the bothersome little brother. The five of us were a team. Then my dad died, and it all changed. I changed. I don't know how to let them in, so I keep them at arm's length. If they knew the truth, they would never look at me the same. I don't want their pity so I can't bring myself to take that step.

"It's my fault, Pres." In so many ways, he'll never understand. "I'm just trying to figure shit out."

"East? That's what I'm here for, man. Let me in so I can help."

His offer is so tempting. So many times, I've wanted to come clean about what happened the day everything changed, but I'm too ashamed.

"It's just something I have to do on my own, Pres, but thanks. What is it you called for?"

He's silent, and I have to check the phone to make sure we didn't get disconnected. Then, finally, he sighs.

"Okay, but I'm here, brother. Whatever you need, I'm here. Don't wait so long ... so long that I can't help you."

Something in his tone has me sitting up taller.

"Is everything all right, Pres?"

"Huh? Oh ..." He clears his throat. "Yeah, sorry. Anyway, I was calling because I have an assistant for you."

Oh fuck.

"Wh-What do you mean you have an assistant for me? If this is some ex-plaything you're trying to pawn off on me because you suddenly have a girlfriend, I don't want any part of it. My life is already a mess."

"No, dickhead. It's Lexi."

It takes me a minute to place the name. Since I avoid family gatherings at all costs, it takes longer than it should. My mother sort of adopted Preston's childhood friends, Dexter, Trevor, and Loki. Lexi is the cousin of Dexter's new wife, Lanie. This is going to be a disaster.

"I don't know, Pres. That seems ... messy."

"No doubt. But here's the thing. Loki dropped her off here after rescuing her from her ex, Miles Black."

I let out a long, pained breath. Miles is bad news. He's part of a crime family Loki has worked for years to take down.

"How is it possible our lives are so entwined with Lexi's family? First Lanie, now Lexi?" I ask, but really it's a rhetorical question. We both know that road can only lead to Loki. And that means I can't turn this girl away.

"What's her deal?"

Preston's voice is uncharacteristically somber when he finally speaks.

"I don't know all the details," he begins. "But she's in pretty rough shape. She's far too thin. She's barely eating or talking, at least to me. All I know is Loki had to rescue her. Your guess is as good as mine as to what kind of hell Miles put her through, but she's family, East. We take care of ours."

He's right. We take care of our family, so he knows I can't say no. It's one of the first things our parents ever taught us. Family by blood and family by choice, it makes no difference. Once they're family, they're family forever.

Searching for my notepad, I ask, "What do I need to do?"

"She'll call you on Monday morning. Hopefully, she'll like you better than she does me."

"Wait, what? What do you mean? What the hell are you getting me into here, Preston?"

His chuckle ripples through the phone. "She seems to be the one girl I couldn't charm. We're like oil and water, and somehow, I ended up having her in a headlock about a month ago."

I sit back, stunned. Not because playboy Preston couldn't work his magic, but because apparently, she has spunk if they went head to head.

"She doesn't like you? Seems like a smart girl."

"She only thinks she doesn't like me. Honestly, we've had some kind of truce lately. But she needs to get back to work. It seems like Miles may have literally stripped her of everything. I just had my shopper bring her clothes because she showed up here with nothing. Nothing at all, East."

Preston is rarely serious, so his tone has me leaning forward.

"Are you sure she's in the right frame of mind to work? Does she know it's an executive assistant position?"

"I'm not sure, but she's extremely smart. She was the number one buyer in all of New England until one day, everything just vanished. They blacklisted her overnight. I have EnVision Securities looking into it, but I'm willing to bet Miles was behind that, too."

"All right. Forget the call. Just tell her to be at my office by seven a.m., and I'll get her set up."

"Thanks, man. I'd hire her in my office, but I'm afraid we'll kill each other."

"And you think my sparkling personality will be a better fit? Jesus, Colton is fucking Peter Pan. His merry ass would be better suited to take care of her." I don't know if our younger brother, Colt, will ever grow up, but his heart is huge. *Unlike my blackened one*.

"I know, but Lexi is a stubborn piece of work who lets her pride run the show. Colt doesn't have any openings, and if she got one sniff of us making up something for her, she'd rip off my balls."

My bark of laughter is unexpected and has me choking

on air. Finally composing myself, I try to speak. "Sounds like she might be right up my alley."

"Jesus, let's hope so. Lexi needs something to bring her back to life. Verbal sparring with me aside, she's a shell right now, and it's fucking miserable to see."

"If she can last longer than my last assistant, she'll be fine. Dealing with me isn't easy sometimes."

"No shit?" Preston remarks sarcastically.

"Whatever. I need to go. I have a shit ton to get done so I can head home for the night."

It's not a lie, but I won't go home until I'm nearly passing out. It makes walking into an empty house that much easier to handle.

One Little Mistake Releases July 1st, 2021. You can order it here!

If you loved this book please consider leaving a review.
Reviews are how Indie Authors like myself succeed.
Thank you!
Please leave a review here!

Avery hangs out in her reader group, the LUV Club, daily.
Join her on FB to get teasers, updates, giveaways, and release dates first!
Avery Maxwell's LUV Club

ALSO BY AVERY MAXWELL

The Westbrooks: Broken Hearts Series:

Book 1- Cross My Heart

Book 2- The Beat of My Heart

Book 3- Saving His Heart

Book 4- Romancing His Heart

The Westbrooks: Family Ties Series:

Book .5- One Little Heartbreak- A Westbrook Novella

Book 1- One Little Mistake

Book 2- One Little Lie (Coming Soon)

Book 3- One Little Kiss (Coming Soon)

Book 4- On Little Secret (Coming Soon)

ACKNOWLEDGMENTS

As always, I have so many people to thank. First and foremost, my family. To my husband who has been our rock even when I'm wondering what the hell I'm doing, I love you more than words can say. To my children who are still adjusting to having a working mom, I hope one day you'll see what I was able to accomplish with my own two hands. I love you with all my heart.

Beth-you continue to amaze me in all that you do. A phenomenal nurse during a pandemic, an even better mom, friend, and human. Thank you for always being my biggest fan and for pushing me when I want to quit. If it weren't for you, I wouldn't even be on this crazy journey.

Rhon: I can't thank you enough for stepping and and coordinating my chaos. You amaze me everyday with your talent, dedication and ability to reign in my crazy. Thank you for being the friend I need, for pushing when I need it and for picking me up when I fall. You are so much more than a PA, I'm lucky to call you a friend.

Kia, Leanne & Marie: Thank you for your unending support. For championing me when I feel lost and for helping in more ways than you can imagine. Your insight and input are invaluable to me. Thank you for being my support, my cheerleaders, my proofreaders, and my friends.

Street & ARC Teams: I am shocked every single day by your willingness to support me. Thank you for taking time out of your busy days to champion my books, to support everything I do, and for being the most amazing teams anyone could ask for.

Jodi: Thank you for all your creativity and helping me build a brand I can be proud of.

Melissa: Thank you for making my books the best they can be.

And finally, to you, my readers. Thank you for coming on this crazy ride with me. Thank you for your support, your encouragement, and your never-ending love for my group of chosen family, The Broken Heart Boys and The Westbrook Boys of Bad Decisions. I couldn't do what I do if you didn't read them, so thank you from the bottom of my heart.

Editor: Melissa Ringstead, https://thereforyouediting.wordpress.com/

Cover Design By Jodi Cobb at Dark City Designs www.darkcitydesigns.com

ABOUT THE AUTHOR

A New-England girl born and raised, Avery now lives in North Carolina with her husband, their four kids, and two dogs.

A romantic at heart, Avery writes sweet and sexy Contemporary Romance and Romantic Comedy. Her stories are of friendship and trust, heartbreak, and redemption. She brings her characters to life for you and will make you feel every emotion she writes.

Avery is a fan of the happily-ever-after and the stories that make them. Her heroines have sass, her heroes have steam, and together they bring the tales you won't want to put down.

Avery writes a soulmate for us all.

Avery's Website www.AveryMaxwellBooks.com

Printed by Amazon Italia Logistica S.r.l.
Torrazza Piemonte (TO), Italy